Breaking the Silence

JM Dragon

Breaking the Silence

JM Dragon

Affinity
eBook Press
NZ

2017

Breaking the Silence
© 2017 by JM Dragon

Affinity E-Book Press NZ LTD
Canterbury, New Zealand

1st Edition

ISBN: 978-0-947528-34-8

Editor: CK King
Proof Editor: Alexis Smith
Cover Design: Irish Dragon Designs

Acknowledgments

Thank you to my beta reader Mel, as always very enlightening, even when I don't want it to be.

Nancy for her studious attention to detail that I miss every time, great work as always.

CK, thank you for your wonderful edit of my book, I hope we can work together again sometime.

Thank you to my proof reader Alexis, darn you find the most interesting things, well spotted.

Thanks Lisa, great job on the final read through.

To my readers, I could say without you I wouldn't write but that would be a falsehood, because I've always written. However, without you I would never have known the tremendous camaraderie of wonderful friends I've made in the years since I began publishing on the internet, initially, and now professionally. Not only did you allow me an outlet for stories that crash around in my head, and for the most part enjoy, but the chance to redefine me as a person when I needed it the most—thank you.

Dedication

Thank you Mel for your continued support in all that I write and beyond. Even when I'm complaining about how difficult things are you are always there with cheerful comments and excellent advice. I'm forever grateful for meeting you and having you as my best friend, long may that continue.

Table of Contents

Also by JM Dragon

The Promise
Do Dreams Come True?
The One
Letting Go
Circus
Falling into Fate
The Fix-it Girl
In Name Only
Death is Only the Beginning
Lonely Angel
Echo's Crusade
A Window in Time
Waterfalls, Rainbows and Secrets
The Dragon's Halloween Collection
Incantations – A Collaboration
Affinity's Christmas Collection 2010, 2011, 2013, 2014

Define Destiny Series
Define Destiny
Haunting Shadows
In Pursuit of Dreams
Actions and Consequences
All Our Tomorrows
Two Steps Forward One Back
A World of Change

When Hell Meets Heaven Series
When Hell Meets Heaven
Fatal Hesitation

With Erin O'Reilly
Against All Odds
Take Me As I am
Echoes of the Past
The End Game
Requiem
Earthbound
New Beginnings
Atonement

Chapter One

"He's dead, Di, get over it." SG Ryan wanted to shake her friend for her stubbornness.

"I can't."

"Can't or won't?"

"It's none of your business, leave it alone, SG."

SG sighed. "I've left it alone for too long—five years too long. It's time to move on, Di, or you will be joining him, and he wouldn't want that."

"Don't be ridiculous, there's nothing wrong with me. I need more time that's all. How would you feel if you were in my shoes?"

Flicking back her hair, SG contemplated that very question, as Di postured her defiance. She had been in Di's shoes, ten years ago when her dad died of a sudden heart attack. She hadn't had to nurse her father and that must have been even worse to watch someone slowly passing away before your eyes and not being able to stop it, but the parallels were there all the same.

"I was…remember when my dad died? Come on, honey, you know you're wasting away here in this apartment. Why not have a change of scenery, and I'll even have the publishing house pay up the rent for three months, what do you say?" Flashing grey eyes turned to her and the sting from them wasn't pleasant.

"I'm not a charity case, I can pay my own way."

SG smiled. "Great, hoped you'd say that, because I'm at the limit of my overdraft right now. I do have just the right place ready and waiting. All I need is a go from you."

Blonde, straggly, shoulder-length hair that had seen better days, swung around as Di became agitated. "What's the catch?"

SG had watched Di descend from an extremely talented, outgoing, and generous of nature woman to a morose, critical, despised and solitary person. She figured no one lost the kind of natural gift Di had, so her talent was still there someplace. Her friend had written three best sellers and been the savior of her small company. Di had been on the verge of celebrity status when her father contracted a viral illness that within three months had killed him and left his only child grief-stricken and in denial. What Di thought were friends and close acquaintances over time had bailed out, and at times she'd felt like doing the same. First and foremost, Di was a friend, and SG wanted her friend back. It was as simple as that, though it wouldn't hurt her business if the author in her decided to write again.

"No catch, Di. Please, for our friendship, take the time out and do this for me. I found this marvelous ocean villa, and I know how you love the ocean. It has a private beach, too, that enables you to keep your solitude."

Snaking what SG decided was a nervous hand through greasy hair, Di's face contorted. "Where is it?"

"A wonderful, small town called Meredith, a few hours' drive away. You'll love it. There's a housekeeper who will look after the house and the cooking when you want it. Let me drive you there. If you don't like it, we'll stay overnight in a motel and come back here. Please, Di, I know you'll love it."

SG smiled warmly at her friend. Even if she had let herself go the past five years, Di was still a very striking looking woman. She had flawless, creamy skin and a strong but attractive bone structure, which made many people turn their heads. Since they had known each other, it must be twelve years at least, she had broken the hearts of a lot of women, and even more men, who wanted her by their side just to look good. Fortunately, she loved Di as a friend. They had forged a business agreement when Di sent in her first novel, that progressed to respect and friendship. Though, perhaps, she'd accept that she loved Di but not in a sexual way. No one other than SG had stood the test of Di's mega breakdown. Maybe things would have been different if she had been in a long-term relationship—something they would never know.

"Okay, I'll go, but if I don't like it, you promise me that I don't have to stay?"

"Promise." SG took Di in her arms and hugged her tight. "Go pack. We'll go today."

"What? Why the rush?" Di pulled away abruptly.

"Hey, I know you. If I let you think about it, you'll chicken out. I say we go now and this way you don't have time to digress. Go get your stuff." SG caught Di's eyes and shrugged. "Have a shower, too, since we'll be traveling for about six hours and it's hot out there today."

3

It was the best subtlety she could think of in the circumstances. Didn't Di think she needed to shower? Even a chicken run drying out after rain smelled sweeter.

"Okay, I'll be ready in half an hour."

Watching her friend leave the room, she sighed. *I hope to God this is a good decision on my part. It can only go two ways, I guess—good or bad.* Placing a call to the agent who was holding the villa for her, she confirmed that they would look over the house today as a potential rental for a minimum of three months with the possibility of extending it to six, which was the original offer. *I think this will be the turning point, Di. Damn I hope so.*

†

SG had prayed that the weather would hold. The forecasters had predicted a changeable day, but when they arrived eight hours later—mainly because of traffic hold ups on the outskirts of Atlanta—they were both ready for a drink and something to eat.

The realtor and SG had been in constant touch during the journey. Thankfully, the realtor hadn't another appointment planned and was waiting for them when they finally drove up to the beach villa. The medium-sized property was well looked after and very easy on the eye. Whitewashed walls, and terracotta roof tiles enhanced the Mediterranean visage.

"What's your first impression, Di?"

"Looks okay."

SG sighed and forced a smile, as she exited the BMW.

A rotund woman with a gigantic smile came toward them.

4

"Hello, you must be Ms. Ryan and Ms. Sterling. I'm pleased to meet you both. I'm Cathy Brown." She held out her hand.

SG took the proffered hand and smiled. "Thanks for waiting, I'm SG Ryan. This is your new tenant, Dilana Sterling." SG turned to Di who gave her a morose look. *Ok. I probably should have allowed Di to make that call.*

"Di, wasn't it good of Cathy to keep her schedule open for us?"

Di looked at the woman and nodded then shook the hand held out to her. "Thanks."

"My pleasure. Meredith is a small town, and we don't have too many new visitors, only those who take the wrong turn." She gave a chuckle.

"Oh, I know what you mean. Some of those signs for turnoffs are a bit ambiguous. I almost missed the one for Meredith and could have ended up going to who knows where." SG grinned, then heard Di sigh. "Shall we take the tour?"

"Of course. I have to say, it's one of our quality properties here." Cathy Brown pointed to the hall, and they entered the villa.

✝

Fifteen minutes later, Di had become bored with the tour of the property and longed to go home. This had been a bad idea. Walking toward the balcony overlooking the private beach, she rested her arms on the balustrade and took in the vista. *Great. A so-called private beach and there is someone dead center.* "I thought you said this was a private beach?" she commented as SG and the realtor came into the area.

"It is. Why do you ask?" Cathy Brown replied.

"Well, unless my eyes deceive me, someone is on this private stretch of sand." She pointed at the beach. "Take a look for yourself." *I'm going home, no matter what crap SG spouts.*

As the agent looked at the trespasser, the only sound she emitted was, "Oh."

"Oh? Is that all you can say?"

"Yes, that is—no. Sorry, it's only Rachael. I'll explain to her that she can't be here. I promise she won't be back."

Something in the woman's sympathetic tone piqued Di's interest. "Wait. You know who she is? Is it common practice for her to invade private beaches?"

"Not exactly. You see, she lives at the local orphanage. She loves the sea, and the current owner of the property gave her permission to visit when she wanted."

"She's obviously not a child, so what is she doing in an orphanage at her age?"

The realtor shrugged. Then frowned.

"Does she have a history with the current owner?" Di stared at the woman who appeared defensive.

"No. Not like I think you are implying."

"Okay, so what's with the woman on the beach?"

Cathy coughed.

"Di, does it matter? She won't bother you. Right, Cathy?"

Di gave SG a hard glance.

"I want to know more." SG pouted and turned to the realtor. "Perhaps, if you could furnish us with a little more information, we might take the rental. Right, Di?"

Di curled her upper lip. "Maybe."

"Well it isn't a secret around here. I guess it won't hurt. Rachael's parents were killed in a boating accident off this coastline when she was twelve. She didn't have any other relatives, and the nuns from the local orphanage took her in. She works as a teacher there now. I'll talk with her."

As the realtor walked toward the door, Di scrutinized the small figure that appeared to watch the waves lapping at her feet. The woman never moved, and the sea didn't appear to want to encroach her space either. It was almost as if they had an affinity to each other. *Poseidon's Daughter. Now where did that spark of imagination come from?*

"Wait. Let her stay. She can come and go as she pleases, it won't bother me."

SG grinned. "Does that mean what I think it means?"

Di turned sharply from her view of the beach and the solitary woman, taking in first her friend and then the anxiously waiting realtor. "Yes, I'll take it."

Punching the air in triumph, SG mouthed, *Yes,* then Di heard her making the arrangements with the realtor.

Di turned her eyes back to observe the young woman on the beach who hadn't moved. Poseidon's daughter. She had to be. With her thoughts churning away, it occurred to her that it would make a great title for a story.

Chapter Two

"I don't know why it matters. Who gives a damn?" The words hit, with a ferocious force, every wall in the acoustic beach villa Di had made her home for the last month. She angrily stalked around the room, ready to rip off the nearest head had there been one. Fortunately for her, there wasn't. At least murder charges were not in her cards today.

Frustration. Her creative thoughts plagued her at night when she dreamed, but refused to come to fruition during waking hours. Di's attempts to scribble anything down even had the housekeeper pulling her hair out at the untidy appearance of notes all over the house. Not that crumpled paper was her normal mode of writing, it wasn't, but when she finally did think of something to write, it was usually when her laptop was snugly packed away. At one time, her computer would have been the center of her world. For the last five years, it rarely saw the light of day. SG had brought with her a new laptop and mentioned that maybe Di should get herself a desktop and leave it always on. That way, when the urge came, she could write at any time, even in the middle of the night.

What does SG know? Her publisher had left her here, alone with all the misgivings and temperamental illusions that invaded her space. Yet she had, with free will, agreed to the move. It sure wasn't working out as they'd expected.

Walking over to the balcony overlooking the private stretch of beach, she decided that today was a good day for a run. Maybe it would spark her muse. As she looked toward the steps down to the beach, she saw the figure of the woman called Rachael who came, almost without fail, at pretty much the same time every day. Sunday was the exception, which surprised Di at first, but then the woman did live with a bunch of nuns. Religion might be a heavy part of her life as well.

Striding purposefully, Di headed toward the spot where the woman stood. At first, Di had figured there must be a mark on the beach that identified the precise point of the accident. There wasn't. The woman stood at the exact spot on the beach, at the same time, just as Di did on the balcony. Was Di a peeping tom? No, she didn't go to that level. It was her stretch of private beach, and she should be able to watch at any time. However, it wasn't anytime. Every day, she took her coffee at the same time and watched the ocean, telling herself that it just happened to be at the same time Rachael appeared.

Minutes later she walked purposely and, with a flutter in her heart, stood beside the silent woman she had never actually met. She barely reached Di's shoulders, and had brown—no chestnut—flowing hair, which traveled halfway down her back, shining in the sunlight. Di's eyes moved to the horizon that appeared to fascinate Poseidon's daughter. Funny how she thought of her that way.

"It's a beautiful day."

There wasn't a reply to her observation or any movement. Hadn't the woman heard her?

"I guess you're the silent type, huh?" Di smiled wryly. *What a dumb comment.* She was stunned as the brightest and most glorious gaze, from deep azure eyes, captured her own. The brilliance of the sun created a halo effect around the woman. Di inwardly sighed. The greatest painter would give his all to paint the conjured sense of peace and tranquility. The poet would pen lyrical prose at the sight.

The woman's eyes appeared to twinkle, as her delicately shaped mouth curved into a shy smile. Di was unable to voice her words, becoming lost in the innocent depths. *Is this like considering the essence of the ocean?* Feeling shaken and disturbed by this encounter, she wondered if the woman was real. Maybe all those years she'd spent in the apartment mourning her father had sent her a ticket to the funny farm rather than this idyllic hideaway. *Oh, God, now I'm definitely losing it. Less than an hour ago I cursed being here at all and now...now I'm a dithering idiot unable to put a coherent sentence together, at least verbally.* Her mind, however, was drumming up scenarios for her to write, and she couldn't keep up with the pace.

"I guess I'll see you around." Di virtually raced toward the villa. Mounting the steps as fast as she could, she made for the laptop and switched it on, praying her burst of muse wouldn't depart before the machine booted up.

Settling into the seat and bringing up a blank document, she penned the title, *In Search of Poseidon's*

Daughter. Her fingers flew over the keys, as the jumbled thoughts vented onto the screen.

†

Dora Drummond entered the house where she worked as a housekeeper, amazed to see the morose current resident of the house doing something other than moping about the place like a lost sheep. The woman called Ms. Ryan, who had employed her, was far nicer. Pity she hadn't realized at the time that she wasn't the one her services were required for. After the initial meeting with Ms. Sterling, she would have gladly never come back again. Fortunately, the woman didn't expect much of her and the job paid well. She would make sure the place didn't go to wrack and ruin, because the tenant didn't seem to care about anything, not even herself.

"Would you like some coffee, Ms. Sterling?"

A mumbled reply came from the writer. Her gaze was glued to the screen, and she began tapping away at the keyboard. Reminded the older woman of her grandson who did the same thing. These computers confused her. What was wrong with the good, old-fashioned paper and pen.

"I'll set a pot going and fetch you a mug shortly." As she closed the door, she was shocked to hear something she hadn't in the month she'd worked for this woman.

"Thank you."

Pottering about the classically modern kitchen, she looked out of the window toward the beach and smiled. Rachael was there at the same place. What a pity it was for her and such a tragedy. She was a lovely person. Rachael could show Ms. Sterling a thing or two about politeness and manners, even though she was at a disadvantage. After witnessing her parent's deaths fifteen years earlier in a freak boating accident, she became mute.

Just as Rachael arrived, she left, slipping quietly away. If it wasn't for the fact she did this virtually every day, you could convince yourself that you'd imagined she had been there. She was so unobtrusive, becoming part of the scenery.

The warmth the young woman emanated had a good effect on everyone who met her. Maybe it might do the same for Ms. Sterling. They say you never know who your guardian angel could be in this life.

Feeling generous, Dora made Ms. Sterling a club sandwich and collected a mug of coffee, depositing a tray at her side as quietly as possible. Her Bob never liked being disturbed when he was reading the paper. Suspecting this was a similar situation, she discreetly moved away to leave the room. Once more, she was shocked.

"Thanks for the food and the drink, Mrs. Drummond, I appreciate it."

She turned and smiled, sure this was a genuine note of appreciation, and saw a returned smile that softened the dour features usually etched in the younger woman's face.

"You're welcome Ms. Sterling." She left the room with a grin.

†

Over several weeks, Di wrote until she fell into exhausted sleep and ate only if it was placed directly in front of her. The muse had certainly come back, full force. Was it five years of unwritten fiction waiting to spill out onto the screen? She didn't know and didn't care as long as it continued. SG, when she arrived tonight, would be amazed that a rough first draft of her new novel waited for her.

Di hadn't seen SG in seven weeks. In that time, she had become a virtual workaholic, except for one thing. Every day at the same time, 12:15 to be precise, she'd grab a coffee and walk to the balcony. There she waited for the silent woman to come to what must be her favorite place on the beach. She wasn't sure if she should invade the woman's space again, but fascination got the better of her. A week after that first meeting, she went to the beach on the pretext of offering the woman coffee, taking two mugs with her.

Those marvelously compelling azure eyes captured hers in a hypnotic gaze, making Di feel like she was out of control, wonderfully so. Eventually, she called it her inspiration. Yeah, the silent woman was her inspiration. Now, every day except Sunday, they watched the sea and drank coffee for half an hour in silence, and then the woman would turn to look deeply into Di's eyes and give her a warm smile, mouth good-bye, and leave.

At first it was unsettling, but eventually, Di found it restful. She had to admit their shared silence soothed her, especially when she was writing a difficult piece of her story. The aura around "Poseidon's Daughter," settled her down, and she usually spent the rest of the day writing solidly.

As the weeks proceeded, Di found that Mrs. Drummond was a font of information about her new friend. Di's heart broke when she was told the tragic circumstances surrounding Rachael and her silence, it all made ironic sense. Funny thing was, to Di, it didn't matter if Rachael talked or not; just being with her was enough. Words didn't matter, and for one in her profession, that was some admission. Rachael's eyes spoke volumes. At least that was what Di thought. Glancing at her watch, she heard the crunch of gravel on the drive. Mrs. Drummond wasn't coming over today; it was her grandson's birthday, and she was helping her daughter with the arrangements. Who could it be?

Opening the door to the 'intruder,' she grinned as she saw SG at the door. "You're early, what did you do, leave at dawn?"

†

SG Ryan was pleased with herself as she looked at her friend. What a change the almost three months there had provided. This was her friend of old, the sparkle in her eyes, the ready smile at her lips, and she looked great too. Her hair was brushed to a silky gloss and had been styled. Not only that, she had put on a little weight. *Mrs. Drummond must be good for Di.*

"Well, hi yourself. Can I come in or are you going to chat with me on the doorstep?"

"Sorry, SG, it's great to see you." She engulfed SG in a hug. The upbeat sound of her voice and the action brought a lump to SG's throat. *This is good to see.*

"I know. I've been missing for a while, but how are you?"

She followed Di into the kitchen and watched her friend put on the coffee and select a couple of jars containing different cookies.

"I feel great, what about you?"

Removing her jacket and placing her overnight bag on the counter, she winked at her friend. "I'm good too, Di. Actually, better than good."

"Tell me more."

"I will. Let's go and sit on the balcony. I've been cooped up in that car too long. The view and fresh air will do wonders for me, and we can trade secrets like we used to."

†

Di picked up the coffee mugs and pointed to the cookie jars. She grinned as SG snatched a couple before picking the jars up and following her out onto the balcony. Half an hour later, they were laughing at the way their lives had changed in such a short time.

Glancing over to the beach, right on time, Di discreetly saw Rachael arrive. For the first time ever, the woman looked toward the villa and right into her eyes. She saw Rachel's eyes move to gaze at SG who was animatedly talking beside her. Rachael abruptly turned away toward the horizon.

A part of Di wanted to leave SG and spend her normal time with Rachael, but that would be unforgivable, and she doubted she could explain away her rudeness. Oh well, it was the weekend and one day wouldn't hurt. Tomorrow was Sunday, and Rachael didn't come over anyway. It was usually the day that dragged on the most, not that she was prepared to admit it to anyone except to herself.

"Is my company so boring you're more interested in the sea?"

Di's cheeks stained red, and she spluttered out an apology. "No. No of course not. Whatever gave you that idea? You chose the view remember?"

SG gazed at the beach below. "Yes, I sure did. It's a marvelous view…I'm pleased you're happy."

"I am. Thanks for finding it for me."

15

"You're very welcome, my friend. Now come on, what's my surprise?"

Di's face cleared of its pensive observation of the beach, grinning as she looked at SG. "You're going to love it, be right back."

†

SG laughed as her friend ran from the balcony. It was wonderful to see Di almost return to the woman she was before her father died. *I wonder why?* SG's eyes turned back to the beach where the tiny woman was still in the same position as she had been before.

The woman on the beach suddenly turned with her eyes traveling once more to the balcony and staring at her. SG squinted trying to make out the features clearly. From that distance, she couldn't. Just then, Di returned excitedly with a manuscript in her hands waving it under her nose.

"You, did it?" shrieked SG as she grabbed for the document.

"I did it." Di passed over the manuscript.

SG turned to the first page and greedily read the first paragraph. "This is great Di, I love it already." Jumping up, she hugged Di close.

"You haven't read it yet, SG." Di's expression glowed.

"My friend, remember, I found you, and I know what you can do. Time for a celebration. Want to go out to lunch—a champagne lunch no less—and I'll spring for it?"

Di frowned then nodded. "Okay. I suggest you have a shower first. I hate to tell you this but you stink."

A bubble of merriment burst from SG as she remembered that was pretty much what she wanted to say to her friend months ago when they first came here. Back then, it wouldn't have been possible, because she was too fragile. Now...now, well... "Anyone ever tell you that your manners are worse than a pig's?"

"Nope." Laughing together, they left the balcony. As they did so, SG glanced back to the spot where the other woman had been. It was empty.

†

"I haven't seen you this happy for, oh, I don't know...years." SG grinned at her friend who was pouring them a nightcap. They'd had a wonderful Mexican meal in a small restaurant that wasn't that popular at noon, although they both suspected the evening would bring a long wait for a table. From there, they had found a bar close to the beach villa. After depositing the car in the villa's drive, they walked back to the bar. They spent the rest of the afternoon and most of the early evening talking and drinking, reminding both of old times.

"I haven't been this happy in...oh, years. Five to be precise. Thank you for making me see sense, SG."

"I didn't do anything, Di, you had to make the big break yourself. I just changed your outlook."

"When you rented the place was there an option to stay longer?"

Smiling, SG gave her a long, exaggerated look. "I think there was some mention of extending the rental—"

"No, SG, I was thinking permanent."

"What? You want to buy the place? I know you like it but didn't know it called to you that much?" SG found it hard to comprehend that her friend would want to own such a place. She had always been a city girl—always.

17

"Yeah, why are you so surprised? For the first time in years—I don't mean the last five but since I can remember—it brings me peace. It's a place where I know I can write and enjoy the process."

"You love the city, all the parties, the groupies, and everything that went with being a bestselling author. I never heard you complain. You always said you could write anyplace and that it never mattered to you. What's changed? It has to be more than the location?" She saw the struggle the question caused while watching her friend's expression. "Di, whatever you say to me is private and always will be."

"It's really weird. I'm not sure I understand it myself, but I've met someone." Di gave a wry smile. "She's different, but I'm drawn to her in an inexplicable way. If I knew what it was, I'd tell you, but I don't. I just know I can't leave here. Not now, maybe never."

"Rather dramatic, Di. I know you writers can be highly strung, but you sound as if you actually mean it."

"That's just it, SG, I do mean it. There isn't anything in the relationship. Hell, the woman's a mute, so we hardly know anything about each other. At the same time, she has an aura about her that brings me so much peace and serenity. It's like all the guilt and pain I felt at my father's passing is taken away for the short time we spend together. I guess I'm not making any sense." Di shook her head before brushing a hand through her hair, giving a spiky look to the short, blonde locks. She walked over to the balcony.

"Is it the young woman on the beach?"

Di spun on her heel at the question. "Yes. How did you know that?"

"Simple deduction, my dear. She was the reason you took the place, and she's become the reason you want to stay.

All I can say is, if it makes you happy then I'll call the realtor tomorrow and find out if the place is available for sale."

"I don't know what I'd do without you, SG. You look after me so well. I often wonder why."

Laughing at the observation, SG ruefully looked to the darkening beach. The ocean was lapping gently at the shore, creating a wonderfully relaxing scene. "Truth be told, so do I, at times. But you're worth it, Di."

They settled into a companionable silence for several minutes, then Di quietly spoke. "Her name is Rachael. She was the inspiration for the manuscript, at first, before it took a mind of its own. I think Poseidon himself had a hand in it when the tide turned each day."

"Ah, so I need to thank both Rachael and the mighty Poseidon for the copy I've stowed away in my briefcase, in case you decide to take it away from me at the last minute."

"I want you to read it, SG. It's different from my other novels— it actually has a happy ending."

"Wow that's a first. I've never known a writer to give their characters so many heartaches in so few pages. Never allowing them an inch of happiness in any of your books." SG winked.

Scrunching up her face, Di stuck out her tongue. "I resemble that remark."

SG let out a small sigh. *Di is finally back.*

†

Later that evening, as Di settled down in her bed, she felt good about the day. Well, almost. She had dearly missed her rendezvous with Rachael that afternoon. Had she been missed too, or didn't the other woman care either way? Perhaps she'd never know.

19

Sometimes, she felt that Rachael enjoyed her presence. Other times, it was like she wasn't there and Rachael was in a world of her own. They rarely moved away from the beach spot that Rachael could call her own. When they did, they walked up and down the private stretch of sand and looked at the shells and sea creatures that washed ashore. It was a relaxing pastime and one Di never thought she would ever indulge in. Yet, she found so much joy in putting the odd crab back into the sea, or listening to the whirl of the sea in a large shell, and wondering where the piece of sea glass originally came from. She'd talk and Rachael would listen. Di knew this by Rachael's rapt expression and intent eyes that never wavered. *Can eyes ramble?* She thought that maybe Rachael's did, but then again she was a writer and fantasized. That was it. Just her over active imagination, inventing things that weren't there.

"I don't know why it matters. Who gives a damn?" As she spoke, that déjà vu feeling encompassed her. Di recalled speaking those very same words, weeks ago. What a different context this was. Previously, they had been uttered in anger, now it was wonder. How strange life was, so many paths, and outcomes.

As she closed her eyes, her last thought was she'd see Rachael on Monday, at their usual time, and tell her about SG. After all, it was only fair to share her friends; she had so few, and they were both important to her. Who knew? Next time SG came over for a visit they might arrange a meeting...on the beach of course.

20

Chapter Three

Rachael hadn't been to the beach all week.

Di wasn't one to assume. Her father had told her, often enough, that wars broke out when that happened. She remembered the only time she had, and he'd reminded her by example.

✝

"You're going to your aunt's, period."

"Dad, please. Aunt Cheryl is boring, she doesn't even have a life. Why can't I stay here? I'm old enough."

Randolph Sterling gave a glance that told her he wasn't happy with her attitude. "Now, why would you think that, Dilana?"

"Oh come on, Dad, she never comes to see us, she lives a half continent away, and I think the last time I saw her was at mom's funeral."

"Yeah, that proves what exactly? You think that means she hasn't a life? I think it proves that she has a rather full life, because she doesn't have time to keep a check on how I'm bringing up her only sister's child. At the moment, she would disapprove totally, and I wouldn't blame her."

Di pouted. "It's okay for you to say these things. I don't know her."

"Right, that's the problem, not that she hasn't got a life. You don't know her well enough to say one way or the other, do you? I've taught you better, Dilana. Don't assume things about people because it's convenient. Say it how it is when you know for sure. Trust me, you will get in less trouble."

Di watched her father closely, he wasn't giving anything away about her aunt either. Another of his sayings came to mind—make your own mind up. Her dad was a great guy. He'd been her best friend since her mother died eight years ago, although now, at fourteen, she didn't really need the cosseting.

"Will you tell me a little about her, please?"

Her father shrugged. "She loves you, for one. Despite the fact that you think she might not, as she hasn't been at the house every touch and turn."

"The odd turn might have been good, Dad," Di mouthed audaciously and was immediately censured with a look by her parent.

"Cheryl is a very intelligent woman. Give her the chance, and she'll teach you things that your old dad never could."

"Is that all you're going to tell me about her?"

"Yep, make your own mind up. If, after the vacation together, you find you still don't care for her, I promise never to foist you on her again."

"Me?"

"Yeah you." Her dad chuckled. "I told her you were one smartass kid, and she still wants to let you visit her." He hugged her close, kissing her on top of her head.

✝

That had been some vacation. Her aunt was not Ms. Average. She was, as her dad said, intelligent and lived a lifestyle far removed from Di's middle-class, suburban routine. Aunt Cheryl's San Francisco apartment was opulent, and she had a couple of cool sports cars that Di's friends envied when she showed them the pics.

The most interesting aspect of her aunt was that she was a lesbian, no bones about it either. Though there wasn't a girlfriend in tow that Di knew about on that visit; she could have been keeping clear until Di went home. The wonderful thing about it all was that Cheryl had opened her eyes to another lifestyle and the prejudice that went with it. There was no pretense that it was an easy situation, tolerated by some, and totally scathed by many more. Over the years, Di corresponded with her aunt, and they developed a friendship that was more akin to sisters.

When Di first came out, Cheryl took time from her busy schedule to help Di tell her father. That was the most difficult talk she'd ever had with her dad, and the great thing about it was he didn't seem surprised at all.

Her aunt moved to Europe the year before her father died, and though they talked monthly, she'd never had the heart to tell her aunt that her father was dying and how she was handling it. When Cheryl arrived for the funeral with her partner, they looked so happy and were making a new life in the Netherlands. Why spoil their happiness with her woes?

23

Di allowed her to think it was just the initial grief that was taking its toll. When Cheryl called the apartment, she would pretend to be happy and say everything was okay, unable to share her grief with anyone. Over time, they had simply drifted apart. She hadn't talked with Cheryl in almost two years.

Now, she was again pacing the floorboards, just as she had when her dad was ill, because Rachael hadn't been around on the beach.

Why did it matter so much?

Walking for the hundredth time to the balcony and looking out to the spot where Racheal should have been, she couldn't help but feel sick with worry. Was she ill? Had she gone on vacation, unable to tell her because of SG's visit? Had something unexpected come up? The questions and scenarios were endless.

Maybe someone in town would know what had happened to her. Di didn't know anyone in town well enough to ask, except Mrs. Drummond. *Yeah she'd know.* She knew everyone in town—it appeared that way with the numerous names and situations that the older woman gossiped about when she came over. Glancing down at her watch, Di saw that her housekeeper was late, by ten minutes, late nonetheless. *Where is she?*

Patience never a strong point, Di practically laid in wait for the woman as she opened the door, pouncing as soon as she came inside. "My goodness, Ms. Sterling, you frightened me!"

Di opened her mouth to speak, shut it quickly, and then shook her head. "Sorry. Do you know Rachael Alderman? I know you do, but how well?"

"Yes, she's a very caring child. Why?"

"Is she ill?" Di heard her voice move up a notch.

"I wouldn't know, my dear. Have you checked with Sister Angela?"

"Sister Angela? Who is she?"

"She's Rachael's surrogate mother over at the orphanage. She will know."

"Where is the orphanage, please, Mrs. Drummond?"

"You know the bank in town?"

Di nodded.

"Turn right and travel a mile. Take a right at Sykes Street, and you can't miss it. The building is Spanish architecture and very well maintained. Did you know the nuns—?"

"Thanks—oh you can have the rest of the day off. I'll catch up with you tomorrow." After grabbing her jacket and car keys from the side table, Di hastily left the house.

"The young today." Dora smiled and moved toward the kitchen. She'd make her employer a snack for when she came home. The girl didn't even know how to cook. What was the world coming to? She'd never find a husband without that skill. Chuckling, she proceeded with her chores.

✝

Fifteen minutes later, Di stood outside the gates of the pretty hacienda. The gates looked imposing, but the actual building was very welcoming. She hadn't known what to expect, but it certainly wasn't this.

Glancing around, she noticed a bell pull that looked as ancient as the building itself. As she tugged on it, the peal made her jump. "Wow, it certainly carries the decibels."

Impatience crunched around on the dirt road, muttering and wondering if it was a foolish idea coming over there. Maybe Rachael doesn't want to see me. She never mentioned the orphanage. Then again, how would she? She doesn't speak, idiot.

Immersed in berating herself, she missed a voice quietly asking her about her business.

"How may I help you?" the voice asked again.

Di looked up at the rather gangly figure robed in the traditional nun's wardrobe. It didn't fit that well. "Sorry. I wanted to enquire after Rachael Alderman," Di quietly asked.

"Are you a friend of hers?"

"Well, yes, that's why I'm here." Di cringed internally at her irritation. "Sorry, I haven't seen her at the beach all week, and I wondered if she was sick?"

"Oh, right. Rachael is fine. Who may I ask is calling?" The nun's plain features were not enhanced when her smile showed uneven teeth.

"Dilana Sterling. I live close to the beach."

"Ah, the author." She clapped her hands together. "Rachael has told us about you. Perhaps it's best you speak with Sister Angela."

The gates opened, and the nun motioned for her to enter. Climbing back into her car, she slowly negotiated the open gates. As she drove slowly past the nun, she wound down the window. "Want a lift, Sister?"

"No, it is a beautiful day for a walk. I'll advise Sister Angela you are on the way. Someone will meet you at the house."

"Thanks." Di rolled down the winding drive toward the house. *Wow, she talks about me. But how?* It shored up Di's sagging confidence, and at the same time, more questions arose.

A teenager with the worst pimples she'd seen on a boy met her at the front door and escorted her to a small alcove. He motioned her to sit on the bench. "Sister Angela will be with you shortly," he said.

How the hell did the nun arrange that? *My car is faster than an aging nun— do they have walkie-talkies?*

"Great, thanks." Placing her hands between her knees, clasping and unclasping them nervously, reminded her of waiting outside the principal's office in high school for a detention notice. *Damn how old am I? This is just a visit. I haven't done anything wrong.*

The door to a room on her left opened, and a nun of generous proportions summoned her forward.

"Ms. Sterling?"

"Yes. Sister Angela?"

Smiling warmly, the nun motioned for her to sit in a bamboo chair that overlooked a truly magnificent internal courtyard streaming with all manner of flowers and shrubs.

The sister moved into the room and nodded as she looked at Di. "You are admiring our view. Although, I say it myself, it is very beautiful."

"I can't get over that this is an orphanage, it's nothing like what I imagined." Di's eyes feasted on the fantastic colors and floral displays that caught her eye.

"Ah, people who have never lived in establishments assume so much and are usually ill informed. We are very happy here and hope it remains so for many years to come. Though funds are becoming tight for us, as everywhere else these days."

"My father always taught me never to assume."

"Then he's a very astute man."

"Was. He was an astute man. He died five years ago, and I miss him very much." The words were out before she

27

realized. Di experienced a sense of relief at the mention of her father. It hadn't hurt as much as anticipated. Her dad had been a wonderfully insightful man, and she missed him acutely; except—this place, her villa, and perhaps the town itself didn't bring her the grief she'd experienced in New York. Perhaps, her healing was beginning

"When you are close to people, their passing can be very hard to take. It is difficult to let go and move on. Rachael has talked of you, of course."

"Talked?" Di frowned.

Chuckling softly, Sister Angela nodded. "Yes, talked. Rachael writes and uses sign language. We have several deaf children who attend our lessons. Are you aware that Rachael teaches here during the day?"

"Yes, Mrs. Drummond, my housekeeper, mentioned it. I wondered if Rachael was okay? I've not seen her all week, and we usually share coffee on the beach around 12:15 every day, except Sunday." Di hoped she didn't sound too anxious and looked out again at the splendid courtyard.

"Rachael has been withdrawn this week and hasn't left the orphanage grounds. A little out of character, I admit. However, she's a grown woman; we can't consider her a child anymore, even though some of us do...me in particular."

Di stared at the nun. They don't know what's wrong either. That's a relief, kind of.

"Rachael is fine, physically, my dear. Would you like to see her? She's currently teaching one of the younger classes, but it should be over," she glanced at the clock on the wall, "in about five minutes. I'm sure she will be pleased to see you," the nun said in soft tones.

"Yes, thank you."

Sister Angela smiled slowly. "Follow me, Ms. Sterling."

They left the room and entered the main corridor.

"My name is Dilana, Di to my friends."

"An unusual name. Is it a family one by any chance?"

As they walked down the corridor, Di could hear the sounds of children moving in and out of various doorways. The whole aspect of the place looked sunny and bright. *It must be good for the kids to be in school with those conditions.*

"I'm sorry for being inquisitive." Sister Angela strode ahead.

Di caught up easily. "Sorry. Not really. My mother wanted me to be called Diana, after her mother, and Dad wanted me to be called Lana, after his grandmother. Guess I'm a hybrid."

"Indeed. It has a beautiful ring."

They passed several doors. The nun slowed as a small boy who was about three feet tall with a mop of bright red hair, freckled face, and a mischievous look in his features stood outside a door.

Di had to stifle a laugh as she saw him scuffing his toe to great effect on the polished wooden floors.

"Sam, why have you been removed from Ms. Alderman's lesson today?"

He looked up guiltily from his toe inspection of the floor, and color flooded his cheeks. He opened his mouth to speak and nothing came out but a squeak. Di had to put a hand over her mouth to prevent a chuckle

"I can't believe this. Sam Campbell at a loss for words. This must be a first. What have you been up to today? This time, I'd prefer more than a squeak or is your voice breaking?" The nun turned to Di and winked before she gave the boy a mock stern glance.

"Nothun'."

"Ah, so your voice is breaking and Ms. Alderman was giving you a voice break?"

"She didn't tell me why," the boy obstinately protested. He looked directly at Di before puffing out his chest. "Are you here to adopt me?"

Di wasn't sure if she should laugh or cry at the question. Kneeling beside the boy, she shrugged. "Sorry, Sam. May I call you Sam?" The boy nodded. "Maybe—"

"I will check on the progress of the lesson. I'll be right with you, Ms. Sterling." Sister Angela knocked on the wooden door and entered, leaving Di with Sam Campbell.

Both eyed each other for a few moments and then the boy gulped before speaking. "Are you looking for a kid to adopt?"

Taken by surprise at the question, Di immediately replied, "No."

The boy's brown eyes appeared despondent. "Thought you might. I'm looking for a mom and dad."

Di felt terrible, as she realized how tactless her no must have sounded. *What do I say to that statement?* "I'm not married, so I don't have a dad figure for you in my life."

The boy moved closer then whispered, "No problem, you don't always need a dad, one parent is better than none. I haven't got none now, and I'm a good boy most of the time. If you want to take me home now, I'll be good."

A deep smile crossed Di's face. She was about to reply when the door to the classroom opened and Rachael stood looking at her with a startled expression on her face.

"Hi, Rachael. Sam and I were getting acquainted."

Rachael continued looking puzzled before turning to Sam with a small smile on her lips. Her hands rapidly signaled her words, and the boy nodded his head. He turned to Di and gave her a cheeky grin before skipping off down the corridor.

The innocent eyes the writer loved to watch on the beach turned back to her, as Rachael simply stared at her.

"I was in the neighborhood and thought I'd look you up. I didn't know you were working. I'm sorry about that."

Self-consciously, Di was looking at the spot the small boy had been watching with interest. She waited for a response, noting the scuffmarks on the polished floor. She remembered that Rachael couldn't speak and that her only way to find out what the other woman thought was by watching her expressions.

Before any more communication on any level could be gained, the door to the schoolroom opened and the children bustled out, almost knocking over the teacher.

Sister Angela was patiently signing to a small, pigtailed girl whose front two teeth were missing. The child was quite adorable in purple gingham that appeared to be the uniform for the school.

"Why not take Ms. Sterling into the courtyard, Rachael? It's beautiful at this time of the day, and I'll have Sam bring you over some refreshments."

As Sister Angela moved past them, she handed Rachael a notebook with a pencil before following the mass of children in the corridor.

Opening the notebook, Rachael scribbled a few notes and passed it to Di.

Do you want to go to the courtyard, Dilana?

Quickly retrieving the pencil from the other woman Di wrote one word.

Yes.

Then slapped her forehead. "Damn, sorry. You can hear me. Yes, please, yes."

Rachael smiled and nodded in the opposite direction to where everyone else had gone. They walked together toward the doors that opened onto the courtyard. Glancing around, Rachael pointed to a wooden bench under an arch encrusted with honeysuckle that was not only pretty to the eye but smelled intoxicating.

"It's beautiful here. I wonder how you can leave it for the beach."

Rachael began to scribble furiously. The beach is beautiful too, very beautiful, I miss it dreadfully.

"Why haven't you been over this week? I've missed you." There it was. She had missed her new friend more than she cared to admit. Something, or someone, must have spooked her. Had she been accosted on the beach on her way home that day they hadn't met up? What if Di had been having fun with SG and Rachael had to defend herself alone?

There was a slight hesitation before Rachael wrote.

I was busy here with the teaching.

"Does that mean that you will be coming over next week? I kind of thought maybe we could have a picnic on the beach. I've mentioned it before."

I'm not sure of my plans yet. Perhaps your other friend can have the picnic with you?

What was she talking about? She didn't have any friends except for Rachael in this town. She couldn't exactly see Mrs. Drummond sitting on the beach with her work apron on, enjoying a picnic. The idea made her chuckle.

Rachael gave her a grave stare.

"Sorry, I was picturing Mrs. Drummond on the beach having a picnic with me. I guess I thought the scenario amusing. She's about the only person I know to have a decent conversation with in this town, except you."

Scribbling something else, Rachael handed her the notebook and turned her head toward young Sam who was carefully walking toward them with a tray. Di glanced across at the boy and winked at him.

"He's a cutie. Bet he gets in trouble with a smile like that."

Rachael grinned and took back the note book.

He is mischievous, cheeky but a wonderful character that you couldn't help but love. Today, he excelled himself by pulling Sadie Jones's pigtails until she cried, and he had to be sent out of the class. Though, I suspect Sadie will play a trick on him at another time to make up for it.

Di read the new note and chuckled. "Yeah I'm sure."

She looked at the previous note.

You have other friends. I saw you with one last week.

Di was puzzled. What friend? Trying to rack her brain, she didn't know anyone else. "Ah…SG. Oh, she's my publisher from the city. You know the city types, they don't stay long in the small towns." Smiling, Di realized that should cover her too, but somehow it didn't. Not now, at any rate.

SG? What a strange name. What does it stand for?

Chuckling, she smiled warmly. *SG is going to kill me but what the hell. She may never know…Rachael isn't exactly the gregarious type.* "Saffron Gracie. My friend went through serious ribbing at middle school, and by high school she decided SG would sound cooler."

A wonderful smile crossed the younger woman's face. This was what Di had sorely missed. The warmth of that smile and the marvelous glow from the tips of her toes to the top of her ears flowing through her.

She has a beautiful given name, her parents must be sad that she doesn't use it?

"Don't worry, her mom still uses it. I've heard her, that's how I know. Otherwise, I doubt that SG would have confided in me."

Sam arrived at that moment.

"Thanks, Sam. Are you out of the doghouse now?" Di gave the grave looking boy a smile.

"Nope, not until Sadie gets her silly revenge." Sam tipped his head to one side and looked closely at Di.

"Do I measure up?" Di stroked her chin. Freckles jumped out at her as his face beamed bright red. Sam stepped closer to Rachael who placed a hand on his shoulder, steering him to place the tray in a safe place.

"Might, not sure yet." Sam stated.

She smiled, as her eyes bounced from the child to the young woman who had a protective hand on the boy's shoulder.

"When you know, please be sure to tell me, won't you?" Nodding seriously, the boy left the two women and skipped off in the direction he'd come.

Di smiled ruefully. "Not sure if I passed his test."

What test?

Yeah what test, idiot? You're not exactly a suitor, just a friend—if only. "Who knows with kids that age? How many orphans are here?"

Di sipped on the fresh fruit drink that Rachael handed her, watching as she scribbled down the next message.

Eighty, yeah eight. We've had three orphans adopted recently. The nuns are not a large order in this area and would take more, but we are filled. Well now we have three places left. Rachael gave a shy smile.

"How many nuns are in this order?"

Fifteen. Many are over sixty. We haven't had any new blood since Sister Agatha, and she was forty, ten years ago. The school is good for not just the orphans but the surrounding area. Many children would need to travel two hours a day for their education if we didn't have a school system here. We have four teachers. Because of the various ages, it is hard to cover all subjects, but we manage.

"Are you the only…hmm…not a nun teacher? Maybe you are a nun. Sorry if I've crossed the line." Di knew that some people were happiest living in an organized establishment. *Could Rachael be like that? If she is, what will I do?*

A bubble of laughter escaped Rachael, and Di's heart swelled at the sound. It made her happy—this woman made her happy. Happier than she had been—ever. Now that she knew that, what could she do about it?

No. Rachael shook her head and grinned. I want to have a home by the sea like your beach house. Maybe find someone to settle down with and have a family of my own one day.

Di mentally ticked two out of three as easy on her side but knew the family part might be more difficult. Sure, lesbians had children but not in what was currently the conventional way. Preoccupied with her thoughts, she didn't immediately reply. When as Rachael's eyes caught hers, she smiled. "I hope you do one day, Rachael."

Both women became silent as they turned to their own thoughts. Sometime later, Rachael looked at her watch.

I must go.

"I'm sorry. I didn't know I was keeping you. I guess I'll see you around soon." Embarrassed that she had kept Rachael longer than she obviously wanted, Di stood quickly.

Coming up to Di's shoulder, Rachael stood. Scribbling on the notepad, she handed it to Di and smiled slowly.

It was a smile that Di thought Rachael used only for her. At least that's what her romantic heart wanted to think. *Get a grip, girl, get a grip.*

Mouthing good-bye, Rachael walked away.

Di glanced down at the note, as Rachael headed toward the main building.

Picnic on Saturday, I'll bring the food and see you at our usual place, same time. Bye Dilana.

It was a fantastic feeling of having wings on your feet as Di left the grounds. She'd securely tucked the notebook in her glove compartment. As she drove back to the beach house, she contemplated that in two days' time she and Rachael would get back to normal. Or as normal as one could when she felt like this. Grinning as if she'd been given the world, Di wondered what *this* was? Who cared, as long as it lasted forever.

Chapter Four

The picnic had been a resounding success even to the point that next weekend she was going to arrange a BBQ and have Rachael bring over the orphans and however many nuns wanted to participate.

Her friend had looked at her seriously for a few moments when she mentioned the possibility, and the more those eyes stared into Di's the more she knew it was going to happen. The warmth of the stare pierced right to her heart, making it thud in response.

The note pad came out the entire picnic. Though Di felt that Rachael's facial expressions could always be read like a book, the written communication allowed them to get to know each other much better. Why she hadn't thought of doing it earlier made her cross.

Rachael prepared a wonderful array of small pies, sandwiches, and dainty, fancy cakes for dessert. They talked for over three hours, before Rachael reluctantly indicated she had to go.

"It's Saturday, Rachael, don't you get time off from the orphanage?"

Rachael shook her head.

"That stinks. You should tell them you want more time off. What is it with—" Di's hand was captured in a much smaller one, as expressive eyes bored into hers. Di's mouth became dry, stopping her in midsentence.

Once more, Rachael shook her head. A wry smile passed her lips before she released Di's hand and reached for the pencil and book. Di felt bereft as the gentle handclasp was removed. It had made her feel giddy at the touch. What was happening to her? She couldn't fall for this woman—she couldn't. Rachael probably didn't even realize that women had such intimate relationships.

I help the younger children at meal times, we are a family, Dilana. Now do you understand? I want to be there, they are my family. It is like going home to dinner.

Not for the first time since she'd met Rachael had Di felt herself jumping to conclusions. Yeah, a family, that would make sense. Why have I been so dumb to assume the worse? Whatever would Dad have said if he were alive?

"I'm sorry, I guess I didn't think that an orphanage would be like that. What an idiot I am." Dejectedly, Di looked at the picnic blanket and the tartan squares that jumped out at her. She wished they would swallow her up.

Gentle fingers tipped up her face, and a gaze that was filled with understanding captured hers.

Maybe the following week, after the BBQ, you could come over to the orphanage and have dinner with my family?

"Me? Are you sure, don't you have to ask the nuns' permission?"

Smiling brightly, Rachael grinned, and Di felt she was being taken on a roller coaster ride as her heart did several unexpected somersaults.

It is my home, Dilana. The nuns accept that I have friends, and they welcome them as any parent would.

"Then I accept. Thank you, Rachael. I'll look forward to it." Beaming from ear to ear, Di felt wonderful as she packed away the picnic items. They said good-bye until Monday and their routine rendezvous for coffee.

Walking into the villa, Di couldn't help but continue to smile. *Maybe someone is looking over me and saying I deserve a break.*

"Did you have a good time?"

Di looked toward the voice from the doorway to the lounge area. "I certainly did, Mrs. D. How are you at BBQ food?"

The older woman knitted her eyebrows together and shook her head. "Not me, Ms. Sterling. I'm a conventional cook myself. My Bob does the honors in the BBQ department. Why do you ask?"

Di frowned. "I kind of promised to have a BBQ next Saturday."

"Well that shouldn't be a problem. Surely you can do that if it's only the two of you. I'm sure it will be fun to prepare the food together."

Wiping a hand over her chin, Di bit her lower lip. "It isn't as simple as that. It's more than the two of us."

"I see. How many exactly?"

Di shifted uncomfortably from one foot to the other. "The orphanage." Di was sure Mrs. D's eyes almost popped out of her head.

"All of them?"

"Yeah, all of them, kids and the nuns."

"Are you mad? That's a massive task."

"Not mad exactly. At the time, it sounded a good idea."

"Well, I think either you change your mind or find a catering company who can help you out."

Di grinned. *Why didn't I think of that?* "Hey that's a great idea, Mrs. D, I'll look in the local directory." As she walked toward the phone book, Mrs. D chuckled and Di turned to find out what was funny. The housekeeper, hands on hips, smiled at her.

"There isn't anyone like that here Ms. Sterling. We are only a small town, remember?"

As the words sunk in, Di realized that maybe she had bitten off more than she could chew. "Damn, any suggestions?"

Mrs. D winked at her. "You are doing a really wonderful thing with this gesture. Let me tell you no one else in town has ever offered, and the nuns help a lot around here. Let me talk to my Bob, he might have a suggestion or two. I'll let you know tomorrow morning when I come by."

Impulsively, Di crossed the distance between them and enclosed Mrs. D in a hug that initiated a chuckle from the older woman who turned beet red and extricated herself from the bear hug. She'd given permission to use her Christian name, Dora, and Di had tried it once; but Mrs. D sounded so perfect for her homely, good-natured housekeeper.

"I never promised anything mind you."

"I know, I know, but at least you're going to try. Thank you, Mrs. D, you're a life saver."

Mrs. D muttered as she went toward the kitchen. "Life saver indeed, whatever next."

Di grinned as she watched Mrs. D leave and walked over to her answer machine. She retrieved three messages from SG who urgently wanted her to call.

Wonder what that's all about? Di pressed SG'S avatar on her phone.

"SG, you rang—actually three times—what's the emergency?" Di held the phone away from her ear as SG shrieked at her. " I'm not deaf, SG, what did you say?"

"I'm getting married."

Di frowned. *I've misheard that.* "Married you say, but you aren't dating anyone, at least you weren't last week. Are you on drugs?"

"Oh, Di, he's wonderful. He's an air force pilot, and he asked me after the second date."

The dreamy voice that came over the line had Di smiling. Who would have thought that businesslike SG would end up a mushy mess? "Second date? Now that's fast work, and you said yes. Where's my pratical friend?"

"I'm still practical, now I'm in love, too, and I want everyone to know. Please, say you are happy for me?"

"Of course I am, silly girl. You forgot one thing in this conversation."

"I did? What?"

"His name and when do I meet him. You know I'm going to vet him thoroughly, as he's proposed to my best friend, right?" A nervous laugh was another first and that made Di grin.

"Darryl, Darryl Lucas. I'm going to be Mrs. Darryl Lucas."

Di closed her eyes. Where was her adamant friend who always said if she ever got married she'd keep her own name, to hell with the traditional stuff. "Okay, next weekend

I'm going to visit, just for a night, no more. Make sure he's there."

"I can't do that, he's due to leave for a mission on Wednesday. You'll like him Di, I promise."

"Then tomorrow I'll drive over and have a late lunch with you both. Is that doable?"

"Oh, Di, of course, and we can talk about the new book as well."

Di laughed. "That's my girl. I knew you wouldn't be permantly stuck in fluff mode. I'll call when I leave, enjoy your day with your fiancé, SG." There was a babble of words as the call disconnected.

"Well that was interesting, who would have thought you could fall in love so easily?" She rolled her eyes and looked out of the window to the crashing waves. *Yeah, who would have thought?*

†

Di grinned as she watched Bob Drummond and an assortment of his friends stoking up the three large, portable gas BBQ's. Mrs. D had come through trumps, months ago, to prepare the first feast for the orphanage. It had now become a monthly event, and everyone concerned enjoyed the get-together.

Di had the distinct impression that the townsfolk had felt intimidated by the religious order. That's probably why this had never happened before. She guessed it needed a stranger to start it, and she thought she'd successfully done that. Glancing at her watch, she had about half an hour before three coaches packed with excited children and at least ten equally excited nuns would scramble onto the private stretch of beach she rented. Hopefully, if SG had news for her, the property would shortly be hers lock, stock, and barrel.

The men categorically stated women had their place, and it wasn't BBQ food preparation. She, for one, didn't need telling twice. She was more than happy to await the masses and enjoy the fare. Not only that, she was given the opportunity to get to know everyone better, including a rather special person.

Rachael and she had found they had much in common but also extremes of opinions that made the relationship a little bit more of a challenge. Each time they "talked" it was a surprise. A wonderfully gentle conversation could go to an all-out attack on each other's principles. No one would know that Rachael couldn't speak if they watched the social intercourse at a distance; she became animated facially and with her hands when the subject was important to her. Even though they didn't see eye to eye, it was clear their bond of friendship was growing daily. Di wondered if her friend ever felt drawn to her on a romantic level, as Di was drawn to Rachael.

Di had decided to take courage to the limit and ask Sister Angela about sign language lessons. In secret. The nun was surprised, but agreeable, and they had begun the task twice a week until she grasped the basic language skill.

Sometimes, she had to invisibly slap herself if she occasionally reached out to touch Rachael's arm or shoulder. It was a temptation she had to stave off for fear she'd act on old impulses and demand more intimate interaction. Right now, Di was more than happy with their relationship, and all she hoped for was that it would last a lifetime, like she knew SG's friendship would.

The phone rang and Di pressed the hand's free button. SG's voice rang out into the study.

"Hi SG how are tricks in the big city?"

A loud sigh was heard over the connection, and Di smiled. Could this be the call she had anticipated but dreaded at the same time? Perhaps dread was the right connotation with her friend's tone. "Trust me, you don't want to know."

"That bad huh? Anything to do with me?"

"Noooo, of course not. You are the golden nugget in my day, girl. How are you?"

"Wonderful, couldn't be better. The kids are coming over for our monthly event. Want to join us?"

"Love to, Di, how about next month? I need to see you."

Scrunching her eyes together a fraction, Di's brow darkened at the question. SG never spent the weekends anymore. She was way too busy planning her wedding to Darryl. "Won't Darryl have something to say about that?"

"What, I need to ask permission now we're getting married? No. It's a partnership, not a shackle on my rights. Don't you think I can live a weekend without him?" The laughter resonated over the line from both women.

"Do you want to? That's more to the point."

"With his job, I have no choice. We'll survive, and anyway, he's on a mission that weekend. Our contact will be nonexistent, which means you may well hear from me more often."

"Oh no, my phone line is going to be engaged all weekend. I'd better warn anyone who wants to call me."

"Hey, girl, none of your sassy comments. What's the state of play on the new novel?"

"Thought you'd never ask." Rifling through several documents on her desk, Di came across her first few pages of the new work she was rather proud of. "Did I tell you I've finally decided on a title you'd approve?"

"Di, when have we ever not approved of a title? Anyway, are you going to tell me what it's about? Every time I ask, you say I must be patient and wait for the draft. I call that mean, keeping it from your publisher."

"I call it building anticipation, myself. I'll spill the beans when you come over next month okay?"

"Sure, works for me. Now, onto the book that's about to go public, *Poseidon's Daughter*. You do know you're going to have to do some signings and publicity stuff, don't you?"

"Do I have too? Can't I become one of those reclusive writers who never have to go into the public eye?" Her voice held hope but resignation as well—she knew the answer to this one.

"Di, if I could get you off the media hook, I would but…"

"I know, I know, it's my own fault. I should never have been so eager for the public eye when I first signed up and had you add that caveat to my contract. When does it expire?" Di chuckled. Her thoughts traveling back to when she had insisted that her contract demand large publicity venues and parties. *What an idiot.* Now she had to keep the publisher happy and do the whole media thing.

"Another two novels and you can do what you want and go where you want, my friend, but I'm hoping you will stay with me."

Di heard the hesitation in her friend's voice. At no time, had she doubted SG's integrity in her business dealings on her behalf. She had been scrupulously fair, cheerfully admitting that she had made a bundle out of the profit margin extracted for the previous novels. "If you change the publicity clause, we will have a deal."

"Sounds good to me, I'll bring over a schedule of events next month. Now, go enjoy your BBQ... oh, and how's Rachael?"

"She's good and will be over with the kids, and the nuns, in I'd say...now actually." A vehicle had stopped on the road outside the villa, and she could hear laughter and shouting from a horde of children. "The kids are here."

"You'd better go be hostess, Di, and I'll catch up with you later. Be good."

"I will and the same to you, don't work too hard."

The connection severed, and Di smiled as she walked over to the balcony and saw one or two children appear. The beach suddenly flooded with many more, and their laughter while running around made her smile grow even wider. As she glanced around, her gaze caught the person she had been waiting for. Rachael came into view. Her flowing, chestnut hair flicked about, as the sea breeze lifted strands for the sun to bounce off, producing a glowing sheen.

Di caught her breath as azure eyes turned to hers, and she grinned like a lovesick teenager and waved. Rachael waved back enthusiastically. Expelling a deep breath, Di hadn't realized she held while her heart was hammering in her chest, she quickly proceeded to join the happy revelers on the beach. *Was she in love?*

✝

Sister Angela watched the interchange between one of her own and the famous author. How different their respective lives had been so far. For the two to meet in this small town and become friends was one of God's miracles, she was sure.

At first, when Rachael mentioned her liaisons with the writer, Sister Angela had wrongly assumed the person was a holiday visitor being kind to the child. Many were toward Rachael, especially once they knew of her affliction and how it had come about. It wasn't until several weeks into the friendship that she found out just who the writer was. Shocked, she had almost broken her vows of noninterference with Rachael's choices. How could she explain to an adult Rachel that she didn't approve of the relationship when she knew little of it? Hadn't she preached that Jesus was persecuted and that they should be tolerant and forgiving of people from all walks of life, just as the Son of God had been?

All well and good saying the words and practicing them when it was one of your own in danger. *Danger? Where did that come from?* Was the writer a dangerous person to be around? She didn't know. What she did know was that Rachael was an innocent, and Dilana Sterling certainly was not. Far from it, if the tabloids and what she wrote about were anything to go by. That being so, Sister Angela had listened intently to every word and expression that Rachael shared about Dilana and found herself growing to like the woman. Unbeknown, the woman she'd doubted had tested her faith.

Her penance for doubt was to read every volume the writer had penned, so far, in her career. Dilana Sterling's books amounted to ten thrillers that never had a happy ending. It was as if the person writing the stories had never reached that happy point in their own life, so how could they write about it?

Her biggest fear, and she hated herself for it, was that Dilana Sterling practiced an alternative lifestyle—that she was a lesbian—and might entice Rachael. Mother Superior, and God too, would probably cast Rachael aside if that happened. Perhaps that had been the challenge for her. People became complacent with their beliefs, as she had, until a stranger entered all their lives and silently cast waves that crashed around them, making them question and, in some instances, change their ways.

In the city, at least according to an internet search Sister Angela had undertaken, Dilana was not afraid to show her sexual preferences. Yet here, Dilana was remarkably low key and didn't mix with anyone except her housekeeper. The very homely Mrs. Dora Drummond, was a motherly figure in the community and happily married to Bob, the local electrician. The only other person known to visit was a young woman from the city, who Dora said was the publisher and certainly didn't appear to cause any suspicion that she was more than a friend.

Probably, Dora didn't even know that Ms. Sterling preferred women to men in her bed, and Sister Angela wasn't going to fuel any fire if it should come out, fearing what people would say about Rachael. Her lovely Rachael was naïve. Petty fingers pointed, given the chance, and she didn't want that to happen, not to one of her own. She was certain she wasn't the only one who had noticed more than a friendly relationship between Sister Matilda and Sister Mary Joeseph at the orphanage, but the order chose to turn a blind eye. If Mother Superior had chosen to ignore the situation, why was it then a sin? Loving someone is nourishment for the soul, why would it matter the gender?

"Hi, how are you, Sister?"

The melodic voice of the writer spoke from behind her shoulder and she smiled back. "I'm fine, thank you for asking."

"No problem. You looked kind of out of it, and Rachael was worried. I told her I'd check on you."

"I'm sorry that she was worried. I was just thinking."

"Ah, communing with the Almighty. Now, that would need concentration." Di grinned.

"Dilana, don't be impertinent." She flicked a smile before turning her gaze to the laughing children. They were hustling toward the stoked-up BBQs, and the townsfolk tending them appeared to enjoy the attention.

"Tell me, Sister, you talk to *Him* don't you? Isn't it a prerequisite of the job description?"

Turning to gaze at Dilana, she noticed the lines around her eyes and the blonde hair, which might have turned white in places. "Yes, I talk to *Him* as you call God. I've never asked, but do you support any religion?"

"Brought up Methodist, but alas, I wasn't approved of a long time ago."

"I see."

"You do? How? Oh no, don't tell me that God mentioned it in dispatches."

"God moves in mysterious ways, Dilana. Perhaps, it was one of his disciples."

"Spare me, Sister, but Matthew, Mark, Luke, and John have long since departed this mortal plain."

"Sarcasm gets you no place, Dilana. The hand of God is everywhere in many of our everyday activities."

Dilana placed flat palms in the air. "Okay, but I never knew the tacky tabloids were one of the disciples. Maybe, I'm not beyond saving after all!"

"I didn't realize that you required saving?"

A hand settled on each of their arms, as Rachael squeezed between the two of them and prevented the conversation from escalating.

"I know, the food is ready, and why aren't I first in line as usual?" Sister Angela chuckled and placed a comforting hand on Rachael's, nodding and leaving them to follow the food trail.

Rachael stared at Di and she smiled, touching the hand on her arm for a fleeting moment in reassurance that all was well. *Did she need saving? No, not any more. I already have been, and my savior is right next to me.*

"Come on, let's eat, you know how you love Bob's chili burgers."

Rachael laughed and rubbed her stomach. Di wondered where she put all the food the housekeeper's husband plied her with.

In deep camaraderie, they followed Sister Angela's footsteps in the sand.

Chapter Five

Rachael watched the children gather their belongings, as they finished the final lesson of the week. It had been a particularly grueling time for the children who were taking exams. Some were for the authorities' evaluation purposes and others for placement in the better schools in the area. Because of the special needs of some of the children, it had been a deliberate policy to educate within the orphanage until they were eleven. Then they would have to move away and join another education facility. Fortunately for the children, they lived within a couple of hours of some very successful high schools. Only the kids with extreme learning difficulties had to be moved farther afield where other orphanages took care of them. It had long been a dream of this order to establish a larger education establishment for not only the orphans but the local children as well. Funds, unfortunately, were thin on the ground, and that idea had long been placed in the archives, dust settling heavily on the game plan.

Rachael was educated in a conventional school environment, until the accident that claimed her parents. She was shipped to several establishments in the space of a year, including medical facilities. Some, she was sure, were mental institutions. All she remembered of that time was being afraid and lonely, shut away in a world that refused to allow her to speak again.

Trauma and shock is what the doctors called it. Over the years, no matter how many sessions she undertook with so-called experts, they were unable to break the psychological barrier that had developed because of the accident. When the nuns arrived, one reached out to her with a wide, friendly smile. She had run like a small child into a comforting hold, safe from the prying doctors, nurses, and do-gooders. From that day forward, Sister Angela became her bolt-hole of security that centered her. It was Sister Angela's comfort and love which helped Rachael become a teacher in sign language at the orphanage, instead of going on to make her fortune in the world. After graduating, she had been asked to teach at rather prestigious schools in the state. Declining them all, she came back to the only place she felt provided her with everything the sea's cruelty had robbed from her as a child...a safe haven and unconditional love.

Now, more than ever, she was pleased she had made that decision. If she hadn't, would she have ever met Dilana Sterling? A question she'd asked herself time and time again. All she could come up with was that their fates had been destined to meet at this place and time. For that she would be eternally grateful. Never having made friends easily, she'd had no one close to confide in except Sister Angela. From the moment Dilana stood beside her on the beach that first time, Rachael had such a connection.

It appeared they were both searching for answers, and perhaps together, they would find them. Their friendship had started out in an odd fashion, gradually creating a comfort zone for them both. It wasn't until she'd seen Dilana's publisher from the city that she realized that she was jealous of what looked like a close relationship. A part of her wanted Dilana as her friend only. The emotion this sparked had scared her so much so that she'd stopped her daily visit to the beach until Dilana made the effort to seek her out.

Rachael chuckled and looked heavenwards. Now, they enjoyed monthly get-togethers for the orphanage, and every Saturday evening they would spend a little time together. They went to movies or the theatre in the next town, and even the occasional meal . Her mind and body finally felt happy and at peace, because of Dilana's influence. Deep inside, she knew this friendship would last a lifetime, and her heart hoped that her friend knew it as well.

Pulling herself out of her meandering thoughts, she smiled as she saw Sister Angela sitting in her favorite spot in the walled, garden area. She had a book in her hands, but it was very likely the nun was snoozing, the heat of the day taking its toll on her surrogate mother.

Although she had never asked directly, she figured the nun must be at least fifty, though she didn't look it. The ravages of age were kind to Sister Angela. She sported only a few lines that crinkled at the eyes when she smiled or, on the rare occurrence, frowned. Rachael collected her books and tucked them in the satchel, which she slung around her neck before making her way over to the garden area. She collected two glasses of lemonade from the jug conveniently placed at the door of the garden. Placing a glass on the small table that split the bench, she sat down next to Sister Angela and smiled. Sure enough, she was sleeping.

She silently looked at her "mother" and gave thanks for this woman in her life. Sister Angela worked tirelessly for the orphanage in all manner of activities, and though she was senior to most of the nuns there, she had refused the Mother Superior's post when their last one passed a year ago. There was talk of closing the orphanage for a time, then unexpectedly, the bishop had given them a reprieve. It was a time to see if they could make the place work without a leading figurehead. No one knew of this outside the nun's order, but Sister Angela had felt that Rachael should know if things turned for the worse and everyone had to be shipped to other facilities.

"You know those lines will mar that pretty face of yours if you don't stop frowning like that."

Startled that her "mother" was indeed awake and watching, she smiled wryly and dutifully cleared the frown from her face. She signed that she thought the sister was asleep in the wonderful late afternoon sunshine.

"Now, my child, let me tell you, I never sleep in the afternoon. I was caught out rather too often by Mother Superior, when I was younger."

The solemn words floated around them.

You miss her, don't you? Rachael placed a hand on the nun's arm.

"Yes I do, she was a very special woman. How they thought I could fit into her shoes, I'll never know." Sister Angela had a faraway look in her eyes. "I remember the first time we met…oh, over twenty-five years ago now. She and I didn't get on at all. Not that you would have believed it from the time you came here. I think, after the first ten years, we decided that sparring wasn't of benefit to the orphanage. So, we put our differences aside and used the energy instead to work wonders."

It certainly did for me personally. May I ask exactly how old you are, Sister?

A deep belly laugh resonated around the walled garden from Sister Angela. "I feel older than time some days, but in years, let me see now—sixty-nine next birthday."

Rachael gasped, automatically placing a hand over her mouth to try and prevent her jaw from dropping. *You can't be? I thought you might be fifty, at the most.*

"Why thank you, my dear, that's a wonderful compliment. It must be the flawless skin. It runs in my family. My mother never seemed to age. I must have inherited it from her."

Do you keep in touch with your family? The joyful expression changed to a frown.

"I'm afraid my close family are all dead. I was born in France and lived there until I was ten years old. My parents were killed in a tragic accident in Germany. My elder sister, Francoise, and I were shipped off to our only living relative, an uncle in New York. He was kind to us. Fortunately, Uncle Ben and Francoise kept me from being intensely lonely. My uncle was religious, not quite a zealot, but close enough my sister thought."

Rachael was fascinated. They'd talked, over the years, about personal things but never this close to the nun's own family life. How strange was that, when in some ways it mirrored her own tragedy?

I never knew you were French, you don't have an accent.

"I lost that a long time ago. I do, however, speak fluent French." Sister Angela grinned.

What happened to your sister?

My beautiful Françoise decided, at eighteen, to go back to France. She was happy and found a nice man to

55

marry. Unfortunately, she contracted breast cancer the first year you were with us and died shortly after. I miss her and her letters very much. We always talked once a month."

I'm so sorry.

Rachael's mind traversed the past and recalled a fragment of time when Sister Angela had been withdrawn and spent many hours with the mother superior. *Was it that time?*

Why didn't you go back to France with Françoise?

"I was happy roaming from state to state. I loved America. I made friends with a couple of nuns on my travels, who guided me to realize that true faith wasn't indoctrinated but soul deep. A month before my uncle passed, I took up the order. He was so proud, and so am I."

I'm proud of you. If you hadn't been my savior who knows where I would have ended up. Will you share more of your life with me another time?

"How about we strike a deal? You share a few of your memories and I'll do the same."

For a few moments, no one spoke.

Okay, you have a deal. You sound like Dilana.

"What do you mean?"

She trades me a memory of hers for one of mine. We decided it might help us both come to terms with our painful memories.

"I think that's a wonderful way of getting to know each other, Rachael. Now, where is the delicious lemonade you brought for me?"

Rachael handed over the beverage. Inside, she was smiling, deliriously happy. Sister Angela approved of her friend. Rachael hadn't been sure before, but now, now she was positive.

†

"I was thinking, SG, if the house sale goes through, I'll sell the old apartment and make a totally fresh start here. What do you think?"

SG blinked a few times, as she considered the question. She hadn't seen Di for a few months, but they had spoken at length twice a week, and she had noticed changes in how the woman's life was moving on. Sometimes, she felt sad because this meant that their comfortable friendship was going to rely more on email and phone rather than direct contact. Although the last five years had been difficult, the strength their bond wasn't easily severed. Now, Di had to make new friends as she herself had done to compensate the loss of the personal contact.

Di had found a new friend in Rachael Alderman, and at first SG thought it was weird. Except, she had done the same meeting and falling in love with a man who was in many respects the male clone (personality wise) of Di. She and Di had often talked well into the night about relationships and what might have been had SG preferred women to men. They were amused when people who didn't know them very well wondered at their relationship. SG hoped that one day Di would find someone to love and cherish as she now did Darryl. *Perhaps, this Rachael might be a romantic interest.*

"I think that's a great idea, and the realtor is working hard on your behalf to persuade the current owners to sell. If she can't, there are other properties in the area, you know."

"Ah, but I want this property. It's very special to me." A dreamy tone accompanied the answer, and SG wondered even more about Rachael Alderman's influence in Di's life.

"Is Rachael going to join us for dinner this evening? You and she date on a Saturday, don't you?"

"She said it was one of the kid's birthdays so—"

"Kids? She has kids?"

"A date? We don't date, SG." The two friends spoke simultaneously and looked at each other, surprise on one face and shock on the other.

"No, she doesn't have any children. I meant the orphans. It's like a family there."

"Right, got it, sounds cool. Wouldn't mind a peek in an orphanage run by nuns myself. Who knows when it could be good fodder for a novel."

"SG."

At the affronted expression on her friend's face, SG smiled wickedly. "Only a thought, Di. Anyway, who better to write such a story? We know, darn well, I can't."

"I can't believe you think the way you do, and for the record, I want to reiterate that Rachael and I don't date."

The force of the word date wasn't lost on SG. Maybe it was time to pry a little more. "Would you like it to be, Di? From the couple of times I've seen her, she looks like a very pretty girl, and you do appear to hit it off well."

Di stood, growling and stalked past her. As always, Di was easy to tease.

"She's beautiful, not pretty. No, I wouldn't want to influence Rachael in any way regarding her romantic choices."

"God, Di, when did that stop you in the past? I remember that poor, infatuated girl at Maxwell's prestigious publicity party. What was it now...your second? No, third novel."

"Don't go there, SG. I was young, she was tempting, and we had a good time for all of forty-eight hours."

"I heard she was never the same again. Her family still blames you for her running off with that girl drummer in a rock band, three months later."

The anecdote seemed to ease the tension around Di, as she settled her back against the balcony and smiled wryly. "I was a flirt, I admit it."

"A flirt? More like a highly sexed vamp, if you ask me. Your female public will welcome you back with open arms when you go on the publicity tour in two weeks."

"About that tour. Any chance we can reduce it from a month to maybe two weeks?"

"You know, I'd concede this, normally, but you agreed to this one final push, especially as you haven't been in the limelight for five years. It will help the sales, and the business needs it."

"Really, well that changes things. I haven't told Rachael yet, and I know she's going to be upset. I'll have to work that out."

Attempting to stop the snicker but failing miserably, SG placed a hand half way over her mouth. "Did I hear that right? When did you get married?"

"Don't be ridiculous, SG. I was just trying to find the right time to tell her I would be gone for a month. Also, I wanted her to know that she might hear about the odd press review or TV interview. Although I don't think she looks at that kind of stuff."

"I think I was wrong when I mentioned a date, Dilana. It isn't a date with you, is it? You've already been roped and branded. I love it. What a picture. This is simply marvelous. When are you going to be honest with me and admit that you care deeply about Rachael?"

A quietness ensued, broken only by the lapping of the waves on the sandy beach below them.

Di wiped a hand across her jaw. "You got me, I don't just care. I'm in love with her."

The words should have a peal of joy about them. Not so from her friend's lips. It was as if she were living one of her own novels with no happy ending.

"That's marvelous, Di. Right? Does she know you're a lesbian?"

SG watched Di shift uncomfortably on the decking, turning to face the sea.

"I'm not sure, we've never discussed it. If she's taken the time to go through any of the publicity on me, it is common knowledge on the net. I've never hidden it or been ashamed of my choices."

"Don't you think that, perhaps, you should tell her and see what reaction you receive? Why not explain your preference in the romance stakes at the same time as the tour? Then she has a month to get used to it and see how she feels."

"I didn't want to jeopardize our friendship, SG. It would break my heart if she didn't want anything to do with me. I think she's quite religious, obviously, living where she does. Maybe she agrees with the church stance on the gay lifestyle."

Walking over to her friend, SG placed a comforting arm around her shoulders and smiled. "Not everyone in the church, Di. How will you know if she reciprocates your love if you don't at least achieve a situation where it's possible to find out?"

"I'm glad I have you as a friend, SG. Where would I be without you?"

"Actually, you would be holed up in that stuffy apartment of yours, eating microwave dinners and being a pain in the ass." SG winked.

"Make sure I never have to suffer microwave dinners again, will you? Mrs. D's cooking is far superior."

"Well—now that you mentioned it, back to business. What have you in store for me?"

"I decided to write a nice, middle-of-the-road, happy story, and I think I have. It's only the first seven chapters, but I think I'd like your opinion before I complete it."

"Girl, you really do love it here. The chance of two novels coming out in the space of a year. I'm impressed. Want to get it for me, and you can chase up dinner while I read?"

"You got it."

Di wandered off to fetch the manuscript, and SG watched her thoughtfully. Rachael Alderman was in for one hefty shock or...not. It all depended on how open minded she was. Living in a small town and brought up by nuns was hardly the breeding ground for enlightenment, but one could only hope in these progressive days.

✝

Rachael had watched Dilana closely all evening. Her friend looked nervous, and the conversation was stilted. *Or is it my imagination?*

Originally, they had planned to have dinner at the beach house, but then Dilana changed her mind at the last minute and suggested they have a meal at the bistro near the house. It was a nice place, casual, and the locals seemed to like it too, especially the younger men who played pool.

Picking up the menu, she selected what she wanted and saw Dilana gulp down her second beer. They hadn't been in the place but half an hour. Something was wrong. *Why not ask? Dare I? It might not be good news and I don't want to lose my friend. Not now, not ever. She is too precious in my life.*

The waiter took their order and returned with a pitcher of beer, instead of a bottle. Rachael didn't drink. Dilana was going to have to drink it all herself and, right now, it didn't seem to be a problem.

Dilana looked up. Rachael captured her gaze and smiled briefly, seeing a spark of emotion come and go rapidly in the writer's eyes. Pointing to the notebook that was a permanent fixture now, she guided Dilana to glance down and read the message.

Do you want to tell me something?

"Me? No, I don't think so. At least, I thought we'd have dinner first."

Is it that bad?

"Is what that bad?"

What you are going to tell me. Is it so bad, I won't eat dinner?

"It's not like that, Rachael. I thought we would eat and then chat, that was all."

Do you need Dutch courage?

"Pardon me?"

I've never seen you drink so much. I wondered if you needed the beer to give you the courage to tell me?

"Don't be silly. I like to have a few beers when I come here. SG and I had a great time last Saturday. It's a pity you missed her, she's quite a woman."

Rachael felt the tug at her stomach as she heard the words. *SG is quite a woman. What does that make me?*

I'm sorry I missed meeting your friend. She's very close to you. Do you miss her?

"Oh, yes. SG is a tower of strength. She's my publisher, sure, but over the years she became a good friend, one who never gave up on me when others did. I owe her my life, at least the sanity part. I think I told you before that she was the one who made me take up residence here?"

Yes, you did, and I'm grateful to her.

"You are? Why?"

She brought you here, if she hadn't we might never have met.

"Oh, we would have met, Rachael, count on it."

How can you be so sure?

"Call it destiny, providence, kismet, or any of the other words you could use. I like to think it was extreme good fortune, but meant to be."

I never knew you were a romantic, Dilana, especially with the books you write.

Both women smiled. Before either could say more, the meal arrived.

An hour and a half later, they were both stuffed and sat at a table close to the pool area. Two of the locals were playing, and others were watching with interest.

Are you going to tell me what's bothering you now? I promise not to relieve myself of the delicious meal.

"Oh, God, Rach, that brought a rather horrid picture to mind." They laughed.

As the laughter abated, Dilana caught her gaze. "You know my new book?"

Rachael nodded.

"Well, it's part of the deal that I go on a publicity tour, you know TV interviews, bookshop signings, promotion parties, the works. SG thinks I have a best seller on the cards, but I'll need to jump start the sales as I've been out of the public eye for a while."

Rachael smiled, then scribbled quickly. It's wonderful Dilana, you have worked hard to get to this point again. It is good news, isn't it?

"Yeah, except it means I have to go away."

For how long? Rachael frowned. She hadn't considered that aspect at all.

"A month, maybe less if I can convince SG that it isn't necessary. The book should stand and fall by merit not with the odd crate of champagne to feed the critics."

A month? Rachael gasped. You will be gone that long?

"Hey, I'm coming back, Rachael, don't panic." Dilana took her hand. "I'm hoping the current owners of the house will agree to sell me the villa by then. I will be back, Rachael, I promise you."

Tears trailed down Rachael's cheeks. This isn't fair. It is almost vacation time, and I'd hoped to spend more time with her.

I know it's important, and you must do what you need to do. Rachael scrubbed away the tears.

"There is something else I need to tell you, Rachael."

Something else?

"Yeah, I guess you were right earlier with the Dutch courage comment. Funny, it doesn't seem to be working."

I'm listening.

"I wanted to tell you that…."

"I'm sorry to disturb you, but my friend over there, wondered if you both wanted a drink?" The interloper pointed to a dark-haired woman at the bar who tipped her glass in acknowledgment.

"That's okay we already have a drink."

"I wasn't talking to you, blondie, but gorgeous here."

Rachael watched the interchange between Dilana and this stranger who looked like she was built like a wrestler.

"You are talking with me though, aren't you?" Dilana stood and got up close and personal.

"Look, blondie, my friend over there is interested in the cutie not you, so cool your heels or I will."

"We are not your type, go look elsewhere, or I'll call the bar manager over."

The woman laughed throatily. "Really? Here in this town? Not a chance, newbie. They need all the patronage they can get."

Just as the woman moved closer to Dilana, the bartender entered the fray. "Any trouble here, ladies?"

"Nope not from me." Di shrugged and backed off from the stranger.

"I told you the last time, I won't put up with you harassing my customers, Rhonda."

Rachael watched the butch woman backing off, her hands raised and heading toward the bar.

"It's okay. It's all cleared up. Thanks, Pete," Dilana answered.

"Great. Those two are troublemakers and hit on every pretty woman who comes in the joint. I've banned them more times than I can remember, but it's a small town and we need the business."

"Okay, Pete, thanks. I'll remember that."

The bartender walked back to the bar and, as he did so, said something they couldn't hear to the two women who immediately left the establishment.

Rachael had been fascinated by the exchange of the last ten minutes and was lost for words.

"Sorry about that, we'll eat someplace else next time." Dilana bowed her head as she sat down.

I enjoyed the meal, and you can't legislate for people like that anywhere you go.

"I guess. Do you want to go home now?"

I thought you had something else to tell me?

"Oh, it was nothing really. Any request from the Big Apple?"

Rachael knew Dilana was prevaricating, but she didn't understand why. Had it anything to do with the situation of the woman who had annoyed them? She would find out eventually. Dilana never lied to her if she asked directly.

Anything or nothing, you know that, except you.

"Anything or nothing it will be, and me too." Dilana grinned.

Chapter Six

SG watched her friend soak up the genuine acclaim, and politely tolerate the false, which came her way over her new novel, *In Search of Poseidon's Daughter*. A wonderful story filled with action, adventure, and a gentle romantic feel about it held the threads together for a satisfying read. If she hadn't known who the author was, she wouldn't have associated the book with Dilana Sterling. It was not her style, at least her old style. When SG had read it in the office, her friend's natural flare for storytelling leapt out at her. What a pity Di hadn't written for several years. However, with the current novel and the one in process, her talent had reached new heights. *Okay, so I have a vested interest both personally and professionally. Even so, the critics are raving over her new book and rightly so.*

Di had been on the tour for three weeks now. The first week had been difficult for her friend. She had appeared nervous and unsure what to expect, initially, but as the interviews and book signings took off, she threw off her doubts and became the old confident writer springing into action. Watching her at parties, SG saw boredom and faraway expressions on Di's face. Her heart wasn't in the city anymore or at the numerous parties she now tolerated. Nope. Di's heart and mind were well and truly held by a quiet woman in a small town, who probably didn't even know she had that power over her friend.

Women, as always, swarmed around Dilana. She was like a magnet. Admittedly, Di flirted, but this time around it was a gentler flirtation than in the past when any woman was fair game to bed.

"SG, please come over here and talk with Di." The shout was the high-pitched voice of Celina Ratford, a patron of the arts having a penchant for taking scalps in the publishing world.

Hmm, it looks like Di is the order of the day.

"Now, what has my favorite author done to make you want me to talk with her, Celina?" SG walked over to the circle of women who were buzzing around her friend. Di smiled at her, as she settled next to the writer's right shoulder.

"She refuses to take up my offer of a cruise around the Mediterranean after her publicity tour is over. I told her she could finish her new book in beautiful surroundings and pleasant company." Celina flicked a finger at her chest.

SG paused for a moment. Celina was around forty, had married and divorced three rich men in quick succession, and now pleased herself. Artistic people in any shape, size, or gender drew her in, as long as they were in the media eye. "Perhaps she has other commitments."

"You're speaking as if I'm not here." Di scowled. "Thank you again for the offer, Celina, I'm afraid, as SG said, I do have other commitments. My next book will be written in the place where I started it."

Di's words were crisp, clear, and to the point, which made the rich woman pout in indignation.

"I agree, it is short notice. How about I stay at your place and watch you work in your environment? You can show me around, and we can become more closely acquainted."

"I don't think so."

"What's so special about this place where you live now? Or maybe it is not the place but a person perhaps? Have you been holding out on us, Di? I was told you were so very…how shall I put it delicately—?"

"Why not say it how it is. You were told I'm easy. That was six years ago. I've grown up since then, and I don't do the bedding rounds anymore."

SG stepped back a fraction at the angry words. She noted the red tinge under the carefully applied makeup on the older woman's face. Celina might be the butt of jokes when she wasn't in the room, but one never challenged her in public. She had powerful friends. *There goes the best seller—crap!*

"You will only be able to market your book on Kindle Unlimited at best." Celina glared at them both and moved toward the drinks waiter.

"How would it be if we all had another glass of champagne and enjoyed the floor show that I've arranged for this evening?" SG placed a hand on Di's arm, guiding her to a safe distance from the aggrieved woman who was now throwing daggers with her eyes. *Glad I have a great suit of armor for these events.*

"That wasn't a smart move, Di."

"Who the hell does she think she is anyway?"

"A patron of the arts and a powerful one. She has friends in most of the large retail outlets, and if she makes certain calls, we'll be lucky to market the book in anywhere but market stalls."

"She can't do that, SG. I thought those kinds of situations went out with the ark and what is this Kindle Unlimited?"

SG held up her hands in a gesture of resignation. Di was right. People shouldn't be allowed to do that, but they did in the print world, and she wasn't a powerful enough publisher to make waves. Appeasing Celina would mitigate any damage Di might have accidentally set in motion. *Perhaps a champagne basket might be a good selection.*

"Not your problem. Hey, hopefully she'll have a few more glasses of champagne and move on to her next conquest." They both glanced in the direction of Celina who was engrossed in conversation with one of the large retailers in California.

"What happens if she does as you say?"

"I'll have to eat humble pie for months trying to get your book onto the main shelves, but we'll do it. No one wants to miss out on a best seller. Besides, there is always the Amazon print option, I'll save a fortune in stocking costs."

"Amazon is more for the electronic version, I want my book held in people's hands like it always has been. How can you sign a book that is in a crazy cloud?"

"Well, there are ways Di. Let me handle that. It's what you pay me my commission for, right?"

Di smiled slightly. "Okay, I'll leave it with you, for now."

SG held her breath and hoped it wouldn't be necessary for her to sell her body and soul to at least give the book a chance to sit on retail shelves. Celina was one nasty bitch when crossed.

†

"When's she coming home?"

Soon, Sam. Maybe even Saturday.

"Can we have our BBQ Saturday, if she comes home?"

Rachael smiled at the boy who was itching to know where Dilana had gone and why she hadn't invited them for the monthly BBQ last weekend.

Perhaps next week, Sam, I can't say for sure. She will be home, but in her last letter she said it would only be four weeks at the most that she'd be away from—home.

"You're a nosey parker, Sam." Sadie Thompson declared.

"No, I'm not."

"Yes, you are."

"Am not, I'm a nosey Campbell, so there."

Rachael laughed at the sparring between the two youngsters. She knew that she shouldn't have favorites but these two tykes had stolen her heart. No matter what happened between them, and there was plenty; she never had the heart to heavily chastise them.

What would Ms. Sterling think if she saw you arguing over her?

Sam gave her a wide-eyed expression and turned to Sadie who had a very similar expression plastered on her face. "Don't tell her, will you, Rachael?"

I won't if you stop arguing and go along to dinner. I'll be there in a few minutes.

"Deal. Come on, Sadie."

"I don't see why I should agree with you, Sam Campbell. I don't want her to adopt me." The girl stomped away in the direction of the dining room, as a red-faced Sam gave a bemused look and scuttled off after Sadie.

Adoption? Dilana? Sam was fantasizing; she would have to speak to Dilana about this little problem. The child could get hurt if her friend said the wrong thing. Kids at his age were very vulnerable, all each orphan wanted were parents of their own rather than a share of affection from so few.

Picking up her satchel, she was surprised when Sister Angela walked into the family room and came toward her, a pristine white envelope in her hand.

"Another letter for you, Rachael. Before you know it, you'll have more written words by a famous author than in her books." The nun smiled warmly.

Rachael grinned and snatched the communication from the nun's hand. Swiftly ripping open the envelope, she extracted a single sheet and frowned. *Dilana usually sends at least three pages. Maybe this is short because she is coming home.* Quickly reading the contents, her smile faded as a furrow formed on her forehead.

"Not bad news I hope, Rachael?"

Rachael listlessly handed over the letter. It wasn't much of a letter, a few short sentences. The content of which was that Dilana had been delayed indefinitely and that she would write back soon.

"Rachael, she's a very popular author, and perhaps it is just another few days. Nothing to worry about." Sister Angela hugged her close.

I don't think she's coming back, Sister.

"Silly girl. She'll be back, Rachael, she will. Didn't she promise you, and when has she broken her promise? You must have faith, my child. If you have faith in Dilana and in God, all will be well."

The words permeated Rachael's consciousness. However, it couldn't prevent the heartbreak she felt. Why would she feel this way? Dilana was her friend, and she had the right to stay away as long as she pleased. She owed no one here an explanation, not even her. Yet, at the same time, her mind reminded her, as her heart beat rapidly in her chest, why it was so important that Dilana should come back to her... I love her.

The tears that had threatened when she had read the letter now cascaded down her cheeks, as she wept for what was never going to be. Her friend wasn't coming home. What was she going to do now?

✝

"Don't argue with me, SG. It isn't about the damn book."

"No? What is it about then? For sure as hell, I don't know why you are doing this."

"I'm attracted to her. Is that a good enough reason?"

"No, dammit, it isn't. I know it's not true and don't you *dare* turn your back on me, Dilana Radolphin Sterling. I know you better, remember?"

A deep sarcastic laugh followed the comment. "Maybe you thought you knew me. I've changed, or have you forgotten that? Wasn't it you who said so?"

"That's twisting the words to suit the situation. You know I meant that in relation to your new life, not this plastic sham of a life you are trying to convince me is yours again. I don't believe it!"

"Okay, then don't, it doesn't change anything. I'm going on that cruise with Celina and there's nothing you can do about it."

"Di, please tell me the real reason. Not the false one you're trying to feed me. Don't I deserve that much? I'm your friend."

SG watched, as Di placed a hand at the back of her neck and massaged the muscles. *What is happening here? Okay, Celina called some of her pals and pretty much made our marketing campaign a nonevent after the party. That didn't prevent her from trying to change their minds. I'm tenacious enough. Di's book is good enough to stand on its own merits and not what some of the big retailers think the public should buy.*

She rolled her eyes. Her publishing company was close to financial embarrassment, and she'd had to delay her wedding to use some of the funds they had earmarked for the big event to keep her head above water. *That is how things work. Not that I've told anyone the financial position, particularly Di. I know Di's views on responsibility. She would view this as hers, but it isn't. It's a business venture, not a personal one. Although, Di will never see it that way. She never has with the publishing of her books. Everything is on a personal level with her, and that is why I will always go the extra mile for Di.*

"I told you, I'm attracted to the woman. I haven't had a lover in over five years, and I want some fun. Call it my libido wanting action."

Sucking in a deep breath, SG gambled on her next comment. "What about Rachael?"

A tornado hit the apartment, or so it seemed to SG. She was suddenly whirled off her feet, as her friend grabbed her by the neck, cursing several times before she set her down. "Rachael has nothing to do with this, nothing, SG. Never mention her name again in this context. Do you hear me?" she growled.

"Sure." Her legs were shaking, and she felt totally disorientated by the viciousness of the assault on her person and the tone in the words Di uttered. *Did she say friend?* Now she had to wonder.

"You'd better go. Celina is coming over for dinner, and I don't want her to find you here."

"Okay—Di?"

"Yeah."

Staring at the person she thought a friend, all she saw was a stranger returning her gaze—it hurt. What was going on here, really? Had Di finally flipped?

"Nothing. Send me the script of your next novel when it's done."

Unsteadily walking toward the door, she vaguely heard a muttered, "Yeah, the final one."

†

Di never thought she would lie to SG, but she had, and she could tell her friend was hurt by the deception.

She glanced at the mirror to stare at her image. She had thought life was looking up, and she was finally in control of her destiny. Then bang, a bombshell dropped on her head and all the preconceived ideas of happiness were shredded into a million pieces.

Why did life have to be so difficult?

About the only thing she had been right about was that this current piece she was working on would be her last. No more publicity tours. No more people like Celina Ratford to get their claws into her, and no more letting people down.

At any other time, she wouldn't have balked at calling it a day and not finishing her current book. Even at the expense of SG's business. This was important...not to her but to the orphanage, and she hoped, Rachael as well.

Yes, she had written the book about an orphanage, and true, she had based some of the characters loosely on people she had met in Meredith, but it wasn't about them. It was more the promise of what that orphanage gave to its residents. She wanted to show the world how important it was and that there were caring places still in existence in this jaded world.

She had already informed her lawyer that ninety percent of her profits on any sale would be set up in a fund for the orphanage, with a couple of clauses. It was, therefore, vital the book had maximum exposure and the chance to sell when it arrived on the shelves. If eventually sleeping with Celina Ratford was the price to pay, then she could do it. She wouldn't like it, but she'd do it. There was a lot more at stake than her current scruples. What did it matter? It was just another in a string of affairs. After it was all over and she had secured the book on the shelves, she would try to salvage what she could of her soul.

As the words floated in her mind, she knew that the one thing she wanted most in life would never be hers anyway. Maybe Rachael wouldn't find out about this slide from grace. Who would tell her, and why would it matter to Rachael anyway? It wasn't like they were romantically connected. *I wish we were.*

The doorbell pealed, and Di sighed heavily as she pushed her fingers through her hair and made the short locks spiky. She turned to open the door to her visitor. As she reached to unlock the door, her heart spoke to her and reached into the pragmatic mind that had taken over.

What if Rachael feels like you do and you never gave her the chance? Will she understand this situation if she ever finds out? Would you?

As her subconsciousness pleaded with her, she opened the door and forced a smile as she was engulfed in the arms of Celina Ratford. She cringed inside and gently pushed Celina away.

"Glad you could make it. I made chili for dinner."

Celina flashed her lashes. "Do we have to eat?"

"Isn't that why you're here?" Di winked, as she bit her inner lip. Thank God, Celina doesn't realize that I can't cook. Maybe the woman will go running to the hills and disappear from my life. I live in hope.

Chapter Seven

Sister Angela gazed at the young woman who sat in the shelter of the gazebo in the walled garden. For all intents and purposes, she looked her usual self, but if you knew her well enough, you could see the changes in her over several days.

No one could have known how a letter could wreak so much havoc in a person, but the one from Dilana Sterling had. Rachael no longer smiled, and the peace and tranquility she'd always emitted was muted to an occasional glow. The young woman had lost weight, too. She had never been particularly fat. Now she was virtually skin and bones, which was upsetting for the orphans who noticed the change in her. Someone had to talk to her. Her dear girl was wasting away, and she supposed, since she was as close a mother figure as Rachael could have, that someone had to be her. Still, a heart-to-heart talk about a certain author wasn't something she was going to relish. These things had to be done though, and why not now. Perhaps, Rachael could move on and forget the writer's interlude in her life. There was only one way to find out.

As she entered the garden, she saw Sam Campbell standing beside Rachael. He was singing her a song. How lovely it was to see the compassion the innocence of the young had.

"Why, Sam, I never knew you had such a wonderful voice." Sister Angela smiled warmly at the boy and was given a rather sheepish grin. He winked at Rachael and then ran off, obviously embarrassed at being caught singing.

Rachael looked at the nun with questioning eyes. She had avoided contact with her, except when necessary, for two reasons. One, because she was upset and didn't want to talk about how she was feeling. How could she, when she didn't know what to say? She had never felt like this before. The second was irrational and uncalled for, but she couldn't help it. Sister Angela had been the one to bring her the message that her friend would not be coming back as planned. Every time she saw Sister Angela after that, she expected another letter confirming her fears that Dilana would never return. Now, with the passage of time that wasn't healing her wounds but merely allowing them to fester, she felt her thoughts were justified.

"May I sit, Rachael?"
Yes
"Thank you child. It's a beautiful day I thought you might have been out at the beach." Sister Angela knew full well the young woman hadn't set foot near the beach since the last correspondence from the writer.
No, I'm happier here.

Clasping her hands in her lap, Sister Angela doubted that very much. She saw the strain etched into the pale features of the woman at her side. Shortly, they would have to call a doctor if things didn't progress with the child. She was making herself ill and for what? "Are you? I thought you enjoyed your visits to the beach."

I've grown out of it.

Smiling, the nun turned to look directly at Rachael. Her comment was rather like one of the kindergarten children, and it made her realize that in defense we often act like children. "Yes, we do sometimes grow tired of the beauty around us. It isn't until later that we appreciate how enriching it is in our lives. Perhaps, with time, you'll change your mind."

Perhaps.

"I promised to take the younger ones to a BBQ at the beach this Saturday. Mr. and Mrs. Drummond and a few of their friends have invited us, and I thought it was a good idea. The weather is closing in and they've missed...well, I thought it was a good idea. Would you like to come?"

Rachael shook her head vigorously. *No* couldn't have been spelled out any louder if she had articulated it verbally.

Sighing softly, the nun looked down at her still clasped hands, as she thought of her next retort. "Sam and Sadie miss you."

Glancing up sharply, azure eyes blinked rapidly in what looked like puzzlement. *I haven't gone anywhere, what do you mean?*

"I'm afraid you have, Rachael. Your body may be here with us, but your spirit has left on a journey of its own. It's breaking your heart and others."

Swallowing the lump that stuck in her throat, Rachael wanted to shout that it wasn't anyone's business but her own. However, she didn't want to hurt the children, they didn't deserve that. It was hard enough living without immediate family, but to be shut out by the only family you had come to know and rely on was worse. She should know that more than anyone. Why did she want to do this to people she loved?

I wouldn't want to hurt them for the world.

"I know you don't. Rachael, perhaps if you shared your burden you might feel better."

How can this ever feel better?

The tragic eyes cut into the nun's tender heart, as they implored her to take the pain away.

Reaching across, Sister Angela placed a comforting hand on top of the trembling ones and smiled reassuringly. "Everything will be as it should, Rachael, if you have faith. Please, tell me what the problem is. I want to help you child, please."

Tear-filled eyes caught hers, as Rachael rapidly hand signed her immediate feelings.

As the child's hands trembled, so did Sister Angela while watching the woman sign. *Why hadn't I seen this happening, why?*

"Rachael, I know Dilana was your friend and you became quite close, but do you know what you're saying?" Nodding, with tears trailing down her pale cheeks, Rachael opened her mouth like a small bird trying to feed for the first time. Still, no words came out into the open. *I know what I'm saying, I love her, Sister, and I want her to come back to me.*

"I understand that you care about her, Rachael, and it's likely you feel—"

No. Not likely. The truth is, I do love her. I feel alive when I'm with her, and she makes me feel whole for the first time in my life. I call that love, don't you, Sister?

All her doctrines said this love wasn't what God intended. She'd lived long enough to know that life these days didn't always fall into God's teachings.

You haven't answered me, Sister. Is it because you think it is wrong and not what God would want?

She closed her eyes briefly. The child was correct. It wasn't what God intended, but that didn't stop it happening. She had to deal with this delicate problem in the best way possible.

"Did you ever discuss this with Dilana?" Maybe the writer had been instrumental in creating this situation and when she had grown tired of a small-town girl she had left, never to return, breaking another heart in her wake. It was the reputation Sister Angela had read about when she had Googled Ms. Sterling.

No. I couldn't, it wasn't something I was comfortable with. We needed to get to know each other better. She said that too. She was frightened of commitment. Dilana never said, but I knew. Eventually, we would have worked something out that we both wanted—I thought we almost had.

Looking upwards, Sister Angela thanked God that at least the writer hadn't been that cruel, though her current absence didn't exactly enamor her to anyone here.

"Rachael, I don't know why she left like she did. Why don't you write back to her and ask if she's coming back?"

Trembling fingers gripped the cloth of her trousers. It's too late. I don't know if she's still at the city address she gave me.

"You could try. If you love her so much, isn't it worth finding out rather than wasting away here, never knowing?"

For the first time in a while, Rachael's eyes shined brilliantly. The trademark smile that felt like you were drenched in sunshine, whatever the weather, that smile creased her face.

Thank you, thank you.

Rachael jumped up, kissed her on the cheek, and ran toward the main building faster than Sam did when he was in trouble.

Watching the exit, Sister Angela sighed. She hadn't committed herself either way on what was right or wrong, but she loved the child as her own. If this would stop the decline in Rachael's health, it was worth bending a few principles to do so. Faith was part of the job description, after all.

Chapter Eight

Di watched Celina basking on the sun-drenched deck of the schooner that Celina had hired to cruise around the smaller islands in the Mediterranean. Di had enjoyed the different islands and cultures more so than the company, and though that was harsh, it was the truth. Her heart belonged in a small town called Meredith. More importantly, with a person there. One who looked to the sea every day and gave Di a priceless tranquility in her life.

Di concentrated on the laughter lines etched in Celina's face. The sun could be a harsh taskmaster of the skin, and she briefly, only briefly, felt sorry for the older woman. In the last month, Di had gone to great lengths to appear interested in Celina but without sex. How many excuses could you make before someone finally realized you were duping them?

In her case, she had help in the fact that she was writing a book. Celina had insisted she be a character in the current book. Di's creative part used her professionalism, making up a fictional tale that she must remain celibate when she wrote, as several of the characters were nuns. *A distraction will be a disaster*, she had told Celina. Di hadn't been sure how that would sound or how it would be received. It certainly didn't sound plausible to her when it ran through her head a million times. Celina bought into it completely and backed off on the going to bed part. Kissing, occasionally, had been part of the menu but mostly on the cheek before Di ran off to her private place to do the finishing touches to the edits. Inserting a minor character into the work had been a piece of cake.

Celina had insisted they take a boat out, ensuring plenty of time to soak up the sun, and peace and quiet for the creative juices to flow. The final edited version of the novel had been shipped last night to SG, whom she had rarely contacted in her month with Celina. She was unable to lie to her friend any more than she had already, despite knowing that SG thought the worst of her. Their limited contact had been polite, making the conversation stilted and one sided. This ruse of hers had worked; her current novel was in every major retailer and apparently selling ten times more than her last novel. There was nothing Celina could do now. Business was business. No one would pull out of a successful venture unless their life was on the line, and she doubted Celina had that kind of arsenal to call on.

Her thoughts returned to SG. The guilt over her continuing deception was eating away at her, but she'd made this bed and it was pointless involving her friend. SG would have argued and said she'd limit any damage and things would work out. There was no certainty in that avenue. At least with this one. She'd mitigated all the fall out and, for only a month of her life, it was worth it. Except. She missed Rachael so much and longed to be with her.

Closing her eyes, she recalled the couple of arty tabloids who had reported she and Celina were an item. She hoped that in Meredith they didn't read that kind of thing, but Rachael might. She sighed.

"Are you okay, darling?" Celina asked, as she placed a bare arm around the cotton-clad shoulder.

"Sure, why do you ask?" She smiled brightly at the woman who smiled warily back and kissed her lightly on the lips.

"No reason. What I want to know is… Why do you always stand at this time of the day, here at the same place, and watch the horizon? There's nothing to see."

A small irritating laugh followed the question, as the older woman sensuously stretched her partially clad body up against Di. It reminded Di of a cat winding around a person's leg and purring in satisfaction.

"Perhaps the artistic side of me sees something out there." Her mind knew what she saw or hoped to see—Rachael doing the same thing on their private beach and wishing the same thing as she did—that they could be together.

"Of course, the writer in you darling. How is the novel coming along? You said it was a short story, and you did call your publisher last night." Celina was now kissing her neck and suggestively pulling at her tank top.

Di pulled away and smiled. "SG needs me back in New York to sign the contract, I figure we can celebrate then. I need to be there for a breakfast session tomorrow. I'm afraid I need to go today."

"Surely not, darling. SG will wait for your beautiful signature. I'd rather we celebrate here, alone, and make love into the morning." Celina wound her arms around Di's neck.

"I placed a call to a travel agent in Catalonia. They have arranged for me to be on a flight to London at three pm and onward to a flight to New York by nine pm.

Celina's face dropped. "What about me?"

Di sucked in a deep breath and gave a tight smile. "Nothing is forever, Celina. You said that at the first dinner we had together."

Celina drew back and gave a shocked expression. "You used me," she whispered.

Di nodded. "As you did me. The good thing is, I did base a character in my next book on you. Isn't that what you wanted the most?"

Celina shook her head, her lips pursed and her cheeks glowing red. She stormed away and disappeared down the stairs to the accommodation area.

"Well that went better than I thought. Now, do I need to swim to shore or will she take me?"

†

"SG, you have a visitor," her PA announced. SG scrambled for her diary to check if she had a meeting at that time. She didn't recall any, but maybe Kate had penciled in a meeting and neglected to tell her. There were none. Besides, it was lunch and usually it was her time to catch up with Darryl.

"Kate, I haven't any meetings scheduled. Is someone early?"

"No. She refuses to speak but passed me a note." Kate handed SG the note. "I told her you were busy, but she's been here for over an hour. I didn't have the heart to turn her away. Sorry, SG."

"An hour you say. Really? How odd. What's the person's name?" Normally, Kate was great at getting rid of the so-called hopefuls who wanted to get in to see her with their manuscripts. This would probably be one of them. *Ah well, Darryl isn't available today so I can make an exception—God knows I need one.* She read the note, crumpled it, and held it tightly in her hand. *Di is such an ass!*

There was silence for several seconds.

"Oh right, yes, her name is Rachael Alderman, and she says she's a friend of Dilana Sterling. What do you want me—"

The door to SG's office opened before her PA could finish her sentence. A beautiful, auburn-haired woman rushed in to her room.

"Rachael, hi. Please come in." SG turned to Kate. "Will you bring some refreshments and then you can take your lunch break."

"Sure thing. Be right back." Kate hurried out of the room.

"Want any coffee or something else? Kate will be back in a moment."

Rachael shook her head and walked vigorously toward her. Her manner changed into a frightened child. Di was right about one thing, the woman certainly showed every emotion on her face. It was like reading a book.

"Hey, I'm sorry to keep you waiting. If I'd known it was—well, you know how it is. I get lots through the door that want me to publish their masterpieces." SG stood, unsure exactly how to communicate with this woman. Di had mentioned a notebook they used. Was that being too familiar?

"Sit down, please and tell me why you're here. That is, if you could explain to me—I think I could do with some help here." She held up her hands feeling like a gauche teenager—disabilities were not her strong point.

Rachael pointed to the pad on the desk.

"Sure thing." SG quickly retrieved the pad and a pen, giving them to the woman.

Kate brought in sandwiches, coffee, and water plus a few other snacks, as SG sat down.

"Thanks, Kate. I have an appointment with Brian at two. Can you call and tell him I'll be late, but I'll be there as soon as I can."

"Yes, no problem."

As the PA left the room, Rachael handed SG the pad before walking over to the small window of the office that looked onto the bustling street below.

SG read the neat writing. I need to contact Dilana. Can you help me? I've written to her several times in the past month, but haven't had a reply. I wondered if she had moved. Would you help me, please?

Letting out a sigh, SG glanced at the pensive woman at her window. She looked different, haggard sure, but way too thin as well. Maybe Di hadn't known Rachael as well as she thought she had. Maybe she didn't realize that the woman did care about her—more than care, in fact. There was no mistaking that fact.

"Which address did you use?"

Rachael quickly scribbled the address.

"That's her apartment here in the city. She hasn't been in town for over six weeks. I'm sorry, she's abroad and difficult to track down. Did she give you her email address?"

Frustration was evident on the young woman's face. She began shaking her head then started doing frantic hand signs before grabbing back the pad to write more.

89

You know where she is. Please, I need to speak with her, its important. I don't have her email.

What should I do? Break it to her gently that the woman she thought the writer was, wasn't that person at all…that she is off on a romantic interlude with someone she didn't even like, never mind love. Damn. SG might not like what Di was doing, but she refused to bring this woman into the triangle. It wouldn't be right to shatter her ideal of the writer.

"I will attempt to contact her by phone, Rachael, but to be honest, I haven't talked with her for over four weeks. She isn't always in a well-connected area. I'll email her as well and explain to Di that you need to communicate with her and have her email you, how would that be?"

Pain etched itself deep in the woman's face, and SG could see why the writer was so taken with her. If for nothing more than to watch the differing expressions cross her features.

Thank you.

SG felt the raw emotion of the moment. Rachel's slumped shoulders indicated her bitter disappointment at being unable to reach her goal. An idea struck SG, as she reached inside the drawer of her desk and pulled out a volume.

"Rachael, I thought you might like to see this. It's Di's current book." The upset woman snatched the offered volume like it was a lifeline and hugged it to her, mouthing *thank you* as she left the room.

My God, Di, what have you done?

Glancing at her watch, she had another ten minutes before setting off for her meeting across town with Brian, her main printer. The second run of Di's novel was due off the press that afternoon. The volume she had given Rachael was a prepress copy and didn't have the final acknowledgments in it. What a pity that was, in hindsight. *I should have thought of that—Rachael might feel a little better if she saw the dedication. After all she had alluded to a special woman who had been her muse for the book.* Still, Di could tell her that herself if she wanted to make contact. That apparently wasn't in the cards anytime soon.

At the peal of her phone, she rolled her eyes, picked up the receiver, and absently said, "Hello."

The voice at the other end had her rocking precariously back in her chair.

"My God, Di, I thought you'd forgotten I exist."

✝

Rachael stopped at the stall selling newspapers and magazines, as she waited for the train to take her to the nearest station to Meredith. Sister Angela had promised to have Rob, the caretaker, collect her when she arrived. She selected a couple of magazines that didn't appeal to her but she knew would interest some of the youngsters at the orphanage. After paying for them, she checked the arrivals platform details for her ride home.

Seated near the platform, she watched numerous people milling around the depot. Some were going slowly and others faster than the trains themselves. *Do they have problems too?* Of course, they must have. *Everyone does. But are they the magnitude of mine?* She wasn't so sure. To her, the complications of her life appeared insurmountable, and there seemed no end to the dark tunnel she had entered. Would the light herald happiness or merely the closing of one door and the opening of another, as Sister Angela would say?

People stopped close to her, and she caught snatches of their conversations, not eavesdropping exactly, as some were louder than others. She realized, perhaps for the first time in her life, that relationships were not simply good or bad—complex. *Yes, complex is the right word.* Rachael glanced once more at the arrivals board, checking to be sure that they hadn't changed the platform and that the train wasn't delayed. Everything was in order, and she walked closer to the edge of the platform. The train was due in a couple of minutes.

Rachael peered at Dilana's novel, clutched securely in her hand like a lifeline. It was after all the only recent link she had with her friend. *How can I compete with a successful career as a novelist? I'm just me with all my faults, but I have feelings. I do.* Her eyes scanned the book's title. *In Search of Poseidon's Daughter. Hmm sounds interesting.*

After flipping the book open, she was about to read the introduction when the train arrived. She quickly stowed the volume in a bag along with the two magazines she had purchased. She would start the book when she was settled in her seat.

†

"Thanks, Brian, you've done a great job. Couldn't have asked for better timing. Ms. Sterling is due back tomorrow."

The head printer appreciated the publisher's sincere comments. She was one of the few he would pull the stops out for.

"Not a problem, SG. I hope you don't mind me asking, but can I have a copy for my wife, Gloria? She's a fan of Ms. Sterling's work. Not my type of reading matter at all, although Gloria swears by them."

"Sure, Brian, take whatever you need. Within reason of course. When I see Di, I'll have her autograph a copy for your wife. How would that be?"

Brian grinned broadly, "Great! Do you think she will?"

SG rubbed her chin then winked. "I guarantee it."

"I'll have them ready for you as scheduled." Brian flicked over the dispatch sheets working out the logistics in his head. "Yep, on time."

"Great. Talk with you tomorrow, Brian, and thanks again. I couldn't have done it without you." SG left and Brian watched as she went down the small stairway toward the parking area.

"Nice woman. One of the best." He turned back to his paperwork.

†

SG snagged the new Dilana Sterling from the dispatch department, since she hadn't any left in her office. She turned the novel over to the back cover. Di's face smiled up at her, and she wondered if she was smiling that expression at this moment. The picture on the book had been taken the second day of her last tour. It was a day before she met up with the disastrous fate called Celina Ratford that took her on an unexpected journey.

The preface had all the ingredients of an old-fashioned yarn that could be applied today. It was loosely based on life. What would the orphanage people think of the book? Would they love it, hate it, or tolerate it, because it was going to bring in revenue? If Di wasn't already on a downfall with her current choices in life, then she wasn't going to be flavor of the month when, or if, she ever went back to the town of Meredith. It was all well and good to say the usual crap about *not based on anyone living or dead*, but would the town of Meredith believe it?

As far as she was concerned, it was Di's best novel to date. Filled with tensions, emotions, and a desire to achieve goals that seemed impossible. At the same time, there was the promise of eternal hope as it ended. Something that was missing from most of Di's books—even her last, which had a happy ending.

As she flicked the pages, she saw the dedication that Di had insisted on, regardless of any fall out from Celina Ratford when she eventually received a copy.

For the woman who captured peace and tranquility in a silent world, allowing me to share it with her. I hope you will include me for a lifetime. Thank you, Rachael.

As SG read the dedication, she realized that she should have waited to send a complete copy to Rachael. She, above anyone, needed to know that Di wrote the book for her. If she could never say the words *I love you* outright, she had tried to do so in another form with her writing. It was the only other way she knew.

Maybe, when she saw Di tomorrow, the situation may not be as hopeless as she thought. After all, Rachael had made the effort to seek Di out. Perhaps the title of the book wasn't such a stretch of the imagination for Di to apply it to herself.

†

"You never told me you were close to leaving. Why not?" Celina asked, annoyed and upset that Dilana had kept that little secret. She had thought they had become close. Admittedly, she had used her influence and forced the relationship, but the writer had appeared amenable to the situation.

"I didn't think you would be interested."

"Interested. You didn't think I was interested. I care about you and want to be your lover, surely that means something?"

Dilana gave her a blank expression.

Celina attempted to assimilate the nonreply. *Have I been a fool?* "I'm a patron of the arts, Dilana. I love your work. So yes, I'd be interested. Have you a copy of the story for me?"

"Not an edited copy. Believe me, you need that, the published novel. I will have SG send you one when it's ready."

"Thank you for allowing me your company." Celina sneered. "You planned this with Ryan, to stop me using my influence on your current book."

"Think what you like. All I know is that SG said the print version is doing well and doesn't need help from— anyone, now."

"You colluded with her. I knew it. That woman is the shrewdest person I've ever met."

"I admit she's a great publisher to have in your corner. She's a terrific friend too, in the good and bad times."

Both women stared at each other. Celina now unsure what to do for perhaps the first time in years. It would be so easy to call some friends and attempt to deliver a severe blow to the book's continued ascension.

"Dilana, please stay. We can be a great team."

"Not possible."

"Why not? We are friends. Surely not everything in the last month has been abhorrent to you." The words echoed on the small deck. "Do I mean anything to you, Dilana?" Celina held her breath for the answer, knowing she had no control. She desperately wanted Dilana to stay in her life.

A coward turns their back when they have something to say that won't be well received. Di knew one thing about herself—she'd been a stupid fool in the past month, but not a coward. *It's time I lived up to the expectations of my family, friends, and most importantly of all, what I expect of myself.*

"I wish I could say that you mean something to me, Celina, but you don't, never have. It was a means to an end and one that you introduced into the equation. I only followed your bidding, since you gave me no other choice. Now, you want to change the rules? I think not. I'm leaving, and you can go ahead and do your worst, because living this lie has torn me apart inside. I don't know how I'm going to convince people that I can be more than the shallow person they have come to think of me. I will keep trying though, to those that are important to me and that I love, until I take my last breath. Because if I haven't any pride in myself, how can anyone else have any in me? Maybe you should ask yourself that same question."

A strangled sob flowed out of Celina, and Di thought she was trying to dredge up anger over the situation. The pained look on the woman's face told Di of the hurt she must be feeling at the rejection. "I can change, Dilana, if you give me the chance."

Dilana shrugged and turned away as the mainland came into view.

If anyone would have told Di this scenario was going to happen, she would have smiled and said Celina deserved every tear and heartache. Now, all she felt was regret that she had been a part of this and an enormous amount of relief that this part of her life was over. She'd never allow it to happen again.

Now, she needed to salvage her other relationships. SG would be her first step and then on to the most important one of all, Rachael. If it took her the rest of her life, she'd keep trying, because now she knew, as she never had before in her life, Rachael was the answer to all her dreams. She now had to wait and see if the hand of fate had any pity left for her and would allow some divine intervention.

Chapter Nine

Rachael stood silently at the same spot where she had spent many years watching the sea. It was there where she had thought she'd met someone who was to become an important part of her life. How wrong can a person be? All her hopes and dreams of Dilana coming back to her had shattered when she read the book that Ms. Ryan, Dilana's publisher, had given her. How could Dilana have written that book and betrayed them all? Was that all they had been to the writer, fodder for her new book? *Even me?*

If she thought that was bad, things became worse when she overheard Mrs. Drummond, two days ago on Main Street, talking to Jimmy Straw, the butcher. He was one of the local men who had helped at the monthly BBQ's Dilana had held for the orphanage. She hadn't meant to eavesdrop, but when the writer's name was mentioned, she couldn't help herself. Her body was like a sponge drinking in every remark, regardless of the content, if Dilana was mentioned.

"You do know, Jimmy, she was cruising around Europe with some rich woman. That's why she never came back here. And that new book—"

"What's with the book?" The butcher carried on wrapping up Dora Drummond's purchases. "Oh, Jimmy, really. It was about us. At least from what I read in the early reviews. She used some of us as character models, and she never had the courtesy to ask."

Jimmy stopped what he was doing and stared at Dora. "Am I mentioned?"

"No. But that poor child, Rachael, is." Dora tutted.

"Now, Dora, you can't go saying things like that if you haven't read it yourself. If Sister Angela heard what you just said—"

"Oh, Sister Angela already thinks the same thing, I'm sure." Dora handed over the money for her purchase. Jimmy shook his head. As Dora Drummond turned to leave the establishment, Rachael scurried away.

The main thing that hurt her wasn't that Dilana had betrayed them but that she hadn't been honest about going away and never coming back. The fact that she had left to be with another woman was simply too painful to think about. Rachael refused to acknowledge the sensation of emotional jealousy it was causing her, though she knew she must face that sooner rather than later. Now, people were talking about the orphanage and her in other than good ways. Not only that, a lawyer was due over this afternoon to talk with the nuns.

Sister Angela had been called away unexpectedly, three days ago, and Rachel hadn't had the opportunity to ask what she knew about the gossip. When she arrived back last night, she had said this lawyer person was coming and that it was important. Rachael decided then that she didn't have the heart to talk to the nun about her problems if the orphanage was in trouble. Instead, she returned to the beach today, which she'd sorely missed. It was the only place she felt a measure of peace. *If only things had been different.*

✝

"I didn't think you would come to collect me." Di picked up her large, canvas bag and followed SG out of the building toward the parking lot level of the airport.

"Yeah, I didn't want you mobbed on your first day back as a celebrity," SG muttered. She picked up the pace and unlocked her car.

Di quickly followed and threw her bag in the back seat, then took the seat next to SG in the front. *Celebrity? She's got to be kidding.*

"What do you mean?" Di asked as SG began to maneuver out of the parking space and onto the road toward the toll booth. "What do you mean, celebrity?"

"Your new book is at pre-order number ten in the charts, and your last book is at two. Seems readers can't get enough of your stuff now. I'm even reprinting the older novels to keep up with demand." SG slowed the car and, moments later, paid for the parking. They headed away from the airport.

Di couldn't believe what she'd heard. "You've been working hard, as always."

"No, not really. You did the hard work by writing some of the best, heartwarming stories I've read in the past five years. I'm being cautiously optimistic here, but I think you might end up with an award or two along the way."

"I don't want to be a celebrity, SG. I want to go home."

"I think you'll be hounded if you don't do at least a couple of interviews about the new book. Didn't you say you wanted it to sell well?"

"Sure I do. It looks like it will without my help. Right?"

"Yes, but anonymity hasn't been your strong point, and your relationship with Celina has only promoted you further into the limelight. Where is she? I thought you and she..."

"No. Please don't go there, SG. Celina and I are no longer together, and never will be ever again."

Sighing heavily, her publisher slowed the car down stopping at a red light. "Do I have to take cover for the fallout?"

"Not this time, SG. Celina promised me that she wouldn't interfere."

"You believe her?"

"Yes. I finally agreed to write a story just for her and not just use her as a character in one."

A beep from behind forced SG to continue the journey.

"You can tell me more of that in detail when we get to your place. I need to concentrate, there are horrendous road works around here."

Half an hour later, at Di's apartment, the coffee pot was brewing and both women sat down on the leather sofa in Di's living room.

"Rachael came to see me yesterday. She wanted to contact you. Why didn't you give her your email address?"

"How did Rachael look?"

"Are you really going through with writing a story just for Celina?"

Both women laughed as they asked a question simultaneously. It broke the icicle barrier that had been present ever since they met at the airport.

"You go first, SG."

"Okay. You're really going to write a whole novel for her?"

"I had a caveat. She has to leave my books past, present, and future alone from her machinations."

"You ditched her, didn't you?" SG grinned.

"Yes, I ditched her. I'll fetch the coffee. It should be ready now."

A few minutes later, Di placed two steaming mugs on the coffee table. She desperately wanted to know more about Rachael's visit but forced her impatience down.

"Here you go."

"Thanks. Rachael looked okay. I think she was worried about you."

Di sucked in a silent breath "Worried about me? Really? I did tell her that I was going away."

"Perhaps she didn't think you meant away for more than a few days. You could have given her your email addy. All she had was your New York address."

Di frowned. "I…did she know about…who I was with?"

"She never said, and I didn't ask or tell her."

"Thank you."

"Don't thank me so quickly, Di. I wanted to, believe me. I thought she should know."

"Why didn't you?" Di's sharp words echoed in the room.

"You hurt her enough by going off like you did. I didn't want to tarnish her image of you anymore than it already was. I've left that final defrocking for you."

"Why are you so bitter, SG? You've made money from my last book, and it looks like this new one is going to make even bigger bucks, you should be grateful to me."

SG stood with anger etching her face. "Grateful? Grateful, you conceited bitch. I put my company and even the finances for my wedding into promoting your last book. I would have gladly spent every dime I had to get you whatever publicity I could to prevent us from being used by the likes of Celina. Then you go sell your fucking body. You want me to be grateful? No way, lady." She placed her hands on her hips. "You have no idea...you never did."

In all the time she'd known SG, and it had been a good many years, the woman had never lost her temper with her. Not even during those trying years of her meltdown after her father's death. Now, she was swearing at her. That was a definite first. Brushing a hand through her hair, she stood to face her friend. "I'm sorry. I didn't know about the wedding money, SG. If only we'd talked."

"I tried to talk to you, but no, you have this massive ego that decided only you could salvage the situation. But at what price, Di? What price did you pay?"

Di watched as the angry and upset SG turned away and went toward the door. "Don't go, SG. Please."

"Why?"

"Because I need a friend, and you're the only friend who knows everything about me and is still here, regardless of the hurt I've caused you."

"I'm not hurt. I'm ashamed of you and for you. You used your body for money. To me that's nothing more than prostitution, and that wasn't the Dilana Radolphin Sterling

103

that I knew and loved. What the hell would your father think? It certainly wouldn't be the person Rachael Alderman thinks you are. How are you going to tell her if she decides to speak to you again?"

"Will you let me explain? I promise you won't think so badly of me." Di walked to within a few feet of her friend.

"It had better be good. Next time you think it is in our best interests for you to sell your soul, talk to me first, okay?" Walking over, she placed her arms around Di.

"I promise, I'll talk to you first. I've missed you, SG. The truth is, nothing happened in the bedroom department. I did not have sex with Celina."

Di pursed her lips to prevent herself from laughing at her friend whose eyes were bugging out.

"No?"

"Cross my heart and hope to die, nothing happened, strictly platonic." Di grinned.

SG moved to sit down and stared at Di. The several muscles moving in her face indicated she wanted to say lots of things but was having trouble finding the most important.

"You want to know how I did this?" Di asked, and SG nodded. "I told her I had to remain celibate and keep in character for my writing. I told her I was writing about nuns."

"And she fell for it, how ridiculous, especially as you were only editing not writing. I never took her for being dumb." SG shook her head then gave a belly laugh. "I would have loved to be a fly on the wall when you came up with that brilliant lie. Never realized you were so devious."

Di contemplated the devious comment and then shrugged. "At the end of the day, she was trying to use me and I turned the tables. She was fair game."

"Okay, so why didn't you tell me this instead of letting me believe—"

"If you didn't know anything about my plan and things didn't turn out well you couldn't be implicated. We both know she could and would do her damnedest to hurt your business." Di smiled, "All worked out, and I can concede the one book if she never sets foot anywhere near me again."

"Amen to that. Well, this puts a whole new light on your time away. Tell me what you need me to do to help get your life back on track."

†

Sister Angela paced her small office area. She'd been asked, once again, to reconsider the role of Mother Superior of the order when she met with the bishop yesterday. If not, then they would consider closing the orphanage and moving the nuns to other orders. The bishop had decided it wasn't good for the order to be without the direction of the post, and she had been given a week to consider her reply. As she had been about to leave, the bishop informed her that a lawyer from the city would be calling the day after her return to discuss a matter of great importance. Beyond that, he'd said little, and she had been fretting about the situation ever since. What a dilemma. There was only one place to go for guidance. Sister Angela's eyes looked up heavenwards, and a slow smile filtered across her face.

Perhaps, the bishop was right and other nuns felt the same. She had been selfish in not considering their needs. If that was the case, she was not the ideal candidate for the post anyway, and she should move on. Though it would be difficult for her to envisage not only leaving but the orphanage closing.

She had considered talking with Rachael but the child had her own problems, especially now. Rachael had left her the new book by Dilana. Rachael had been upset by the content, so Sister Angela had read it with great interest.

Yes, the writer had taken liberties in using certain aspects of the town and the orphanage to form the idea of the novel, but it was beautifully written and captured the essence of what they had, over the years, hoped to achieve. Here indeed, was a book that believed in faith and hope at its core. No one could fail to enjoy the drama of the characters' lives, and it had every element within its bindings.

When all this was over with the lawyer, she would sit down with Rachael and find out exactly what she was feeling about the writer. It was apparently common knowledge, or rather gossip, in town that Dilana had left for a trip abroad with another woman friend. Those that hadn't known the author was a lesbian, soon did. The gossips began their busybody tactics of informing everyone who wanted to know and even those who didn't. The worse thing was they had begun to talk about Rachael, wondering if the writer had corrupted her into the lesbian way of life. Perhaps corrupted was a little harsh, but then life was, never more so than now.

Walking over to the window, she looked out and saw three of the older nuns. Sister Josie was ninety-one, Sister Carolina eighty-five, and Sister Angelina seventy-three. They still helped, especially in the cooking and gardening areas, and the children loved them. How could she see them placed in another order? It wouldn't be fair after all they had committed to the community over the years and calling this place their final home. She had the ability to prevent it. Had she faith in herself to be the head of the order? At this moment, she didn't think so.

Perhaps, it was time to have a "family" meeting and discuss her current situation with the other nuns. After all, it was their lives too.

✝

Celina Ratford picked up the volume on her coffee table. The evening before, she'd had a rather boisterous homecoming party. Many of the people she kept around for fun attended. Now, after her own enlightenment over the last few weeks with Dilana Sterling, she considered them merely hangers on. Her headache fueled by the alcohol she had consumed the night before left her mouth feeling like a brewer's waste.

She wondered who had left her this gem last night because it hadn't been there before. She scanned the title and author's name.

When Dreams Need the Hand of Faith by D R Sterling.

The name alone sent shivers down Celina's back and she frowned. Sucking in a deep breath, she turned the first few pages and closed her eyes in pain as she read the dedication.

For the woman who captured peace and tranquility in a silent world, allowing me to share it with her. I hope you will include me for a lifetime. Thank you, Rachael.

That was why Dilana hadn't wanted to stay with her. She was already in love with someone else. Had she meant nothing to the author? What of this other woman? Hadn't she cared about Dilana spending alone time with her?

107

Too many questions and no satisfactory answers. Sitting down heavily on one of the plush sofas in the room, she put her head in her hands. She knew that she ultimately deserved the author's lack of emotional commitment. How could it have been any other way when she had blackmailed her? In the beginning, anyway. Her heart had hoped that, over time, Dilana would come to care for her—no, love her, as she had fallen in love with Di. That wasn't to be and obviously never had been an option. There were several options open to her but which to choose—which indeed.

Chapter Ten

It was her favorite time of the day. The one she called her "Rachael spotting time." Others watched birds, animals, or the stars. She watched for a wonderful person called Rachael Alderman. Di helped herself to a cup of coffee the housekeeper had made. It was unusually bitter, and she grimaced at the taste. She guessed that good old Mrs. D wanted to poison her with the unhappy beverage. Well, maybe the woman had reason for the grouse, though not as much as Rachael had. All she hoped for was that Rachael would let her speak with her for a short time.

As usual, SG had been her rock, since she arrived back in Meredith a month earlier. Di knew she didn't deserve such a friend, but appreciated how lucky she was to have one. This time around, she was going to make sure she didn't screw it up. Her first task toward redemption with her friend had been to agree to three talk shows and ten book signings in the next month. One proviso—no parties or any social gatherings afterwards. Having learned her lesson, she wasn't going to have temptation put in her way ever again. Not that she had been tempted before. Circumstances had prevailed in such a way to give her reasons for taking the action she did. The reasons were noble, however she had been unwise.

Walking toward the balcony, she was stopped before she could venture out and see if the vision in her dreams was there, as she usually was. *Please, please let her be there.*

"Ms. Sterling?"

Surprised by the sound, Di turned quickly at the cold tone from Mrs. D. "Yes?"

"You should leave well enough alone." The housekeeper had her hands folded across her chest. The pose reminded Di of old, British school movies and the reproving head teachers that the boisterous girls always ended up being brought in front of for misdeeds.

"I'm sorry, Mrs. D, run that one by me again?"

"I'm talking about Rachael. She's not one of your types."

There it was again, the admonishing tone. *Yikes, I'm in big trouble here, for sure.* "Exactly how has Rachael entered into the conversation? Unless I'm mistaken, she's not in the room with us, is she?" *Oh, I know exactly what you're saying, Mrs. D, disapproval is painted all over your face.*

"No, she isn't, she's on the beach, and you are going to try and talk with her after abandoning her for weeks for some rich widow. If I was her, I wouldn't want to see you again."

Di was flabbergasted at the comment. Okay, she knew that they might know about her leaving without a proper good-bye, but what the hell was this about a rich widow? Crap, did they Google her? She didn't think Mrs. D trusted computers. "Not that it's any of your business, but why would you say such a thing?"

110

Mrs. D remained in her rigid stance. "It's common knowledge on the entertainment channel. I must say, I don't like your choice of companions. Our Rachael is far superior in every way."

Di didn't know if she should laugh or cry at the comment. At first, she had assumed that the woman hadn't approved of her lifestyle, but it wasn't that at all. She was disapproving because Di had left Rachael in the lurch to go off with a supposed celebrity stranger—hell, how complicated can it get?

"Okay, I'm confused here. In one breath, you say Rachael isn't my type, in the next you say I was better off with her. Kind of a contradiction in terms, Mrs. D?"

Walking closer to her, the housekeeper jabbed a finger right into her chest.

"Hey, that hurt."

"I'd give your hide a tanning if I thought it would do any good. Let me tell you one thing, Ms. Famous Writer Sterling, *our* Rachael is far superior in all ways to you and those strange people you end up with." Mrs. D narrowed her eyes and let out a little growl. "And, she was a married woman too."

"Hold it, hold it. This is a stupid conversation. You've been listening to the crappy tabloids."

"No, it's the truth. Maggie Shore's column is never wrong. If I wasn't such a gossip myself, I'd let you tell me all the juicy details."

Di snorted trying to prevent her laughter from brimming over. Not even in her drunken, early writing times could she have ever imagined this kind of dialogue with anyone. Not even her characters. Yet here she was, in life, doing just that. How weird.

"A gossip huh? Then shall we get the story straight from the horse's mouth? I'm a lesbian, proud to be and happy with my lifestyle choice. I'm human too, and that means I make mistakes like everyone else. I have had relationships that didn't work out just like anyone. What I've found out is that if I'm lucky, I might still retain my friends, and that's exactly who Rachael is. My friend. Nothing more."

There. It was said. No way did she want anyone in Meredith making up lies about Rachael. She didn't deserve it. They were friends or had been, nothing more. A thought niggled at her though—*why did Mrs. D think differently?* The blustering, that came next was comical.

"Well, I knew that, of course I did. Our Rachael is a God-fearing person brought up by nuns."

Shaking her head slightly, Di had to wonder at the housekeeper's naivety. Di glanced at her watch. "Absolutely, Mrs. D. Now, is it okay if I see if she's there? I wanted a quick word with her. It's been a while."

"Oh, she left the beach, Ms. Sterling. She was walking away as I came into the room."

If Di was capable of murder she would have done it right there and then. Fortunately for Mrs. D, that element wasn't part of her makeup. "Thanks for that." Di walked over to the balcony and looked out. Maybe Rachael hadn't left, just moved further up the beach—yeah, right.

She looked at the familiar view that had been her only hold onto the life she craved when she was away. Except one thing was missing, the most important ingredient. Rachael. Di glanced at her watch. Then turned back into the room. "I'm going to get ready, or I'll be late for a meeting I've scheduled in town. Hopefully, I'll be back before you go home." She headed to her room to change.

112

†

Sam watched the arrival of a sleek, black vehicle traveling up the long drive to the orphanage, his eyes wide.

"Are you going to see who it is, Sam?" Sadie asked, as she pushed the boy toward the edge, closer to the drive. They had been hiding behind the hedge waiting to see the lawyer that Sister Angela had said was very important and that they had to behave. Now that was like a red rag to a bull, not just for Sam, Sadie too.

"I will. I will. No pressure," the boy said and hung back.

"Want me to do it?" Sadie's pigtails were swinging, and her smile showed braces over her teeth.

"You can't do it. You're a girl."

Sadie's face went red, and she growled as she squared up to him. "You are a dimwit, Sam. Don't you know by now that girls rule?" It was a fact, they lived with nuns.

"I'm not a dimwit, and boys are as good as girls any day…better even."

"I'll open the door, cowardly custard, cowardly custard, Sam Campbell," Sadie chanted and was given a scowl as Sam's attention was drawn by the car pulling up outside the doors of the orphanage.

"I'm not a coward, so there," Sam said.

"Prove it."

Sam scrunched up his face at the challenge. He would. "I will." Puffing out his chest, he moved from behind the hedge and walked toward the stationary car. He gave Sadie a backward glance.

Sadie crossed her arms and grinned.

Sam returned to his quarry and ran toward the car.

The door opened, and a large man in a black suit got out of the driver's door.

Sam ran fearlessly toward the man, awestruck by his size. "Are you the lawyer?"

A gruff, deep voice answered, "No." The large man, who looked like a giant to Sam, walked around the vehicle and opened the door to the passenger section.

Sam followed and his jaw dropped.

†

Rachael eventually walked back toward the orphanage by the "secret" route all the orphans knew. By diverting from the main road and through the town, a side track took her through Pool's field and along the creek bordering the two acres of the nunnery and its associated buildings. Not many used the old path these days, except for her and, she suspected, Sam and Sadie. Those two reminded her of when she was a teenager growing up here. She would sneak off without the nuns' knowledge and end up on the beach.

The two youngsters hadn't ever made it to the beach that she knew of, but they did love to tease old man Pool's prize bull in the adjoining field to the one they crossed. One of these days, the bull would catch up with the two kids. Though, how could she repress the adventuresome spirit in a child with fewer advantages than those with a family? She suspected that was why the nuns turned the odd blind eye to their activities.

Rachael climbed over the stile through a giant, ten-foot-tall thicket hedge surrounding the only place she called home. She heard activity behind the smaller hedge leading to the drive and knew those voices very well. Sadie and Sam.

Smiling, she wondered what they could possibly be up to now. Glancing at her wristwatch, she smiled as she realized that the lawyer was probably here or due to arrive soon. Strangers always caused extreme interest in the children. After leaving the beach, she had sat by the creek for over an hour, contemplating her life and the future it held for her, before deciding to venture back. Time and faith would show her the way forward, but she was unsure that God would have a hand in it, considering her motivations.

Increasing her pace, she came upon the drive and saw a large, black car standing on the gravel drive. A well-dressed man held the passenger door open. From her position, she could see what was going on, but they couldn't see her. That was a useful tactic for knowing the secrets of the orphanage grounds—you never knew when you might need the obscurity.

Her smile widened, as she spotted Sadie hanging back in the hedge to her left and Sam standing very close to the man holding the car door. This must be the lawyer. Who else were they expecting, and when did anyone ever drive up in a limousine?

She watched a slight man, no taller than herself, climb out of the back. He was dressed in a pin-striped, charcoal suit, giving him a grander stature than his height ever would. A black, leather briefcase was clasped in his hand, as he looked toward the building in front of him.

Expecting the door of the vehicle to be closed behind him, she was surprised to see another person climb out. Her jaw dropped to the floor as she recognized the other passenger.

Dilana Sterling.

Rachael watched, rooted to the spot, as Dilana stood beside the lawyer. Sam approached and moved closer to

Dilana. He looked tiny in comparison to the three adults standing on the hard drive. She strained her hearing toward the voices of Sam and Dilana but couldn't hear the conversation.

†

"Hi, Sam, are you the welcoming committee?" Dilana's lips twitched at the large, saucer eyes staring at her.

"You came back."

Di gave the boy a long look. He was angry. She could hear the accusation in his tone. She hadn't realized her going away would be upsetting to any of the children. Inwardly, she shook her head. *God, what a fool I was.* "Yes, Sam, I came back. How are you?" Her reply was cordial with what she hoped would impart a notion of respect. It worked. Sam puffed out his chest and smiled at her.

"I'm good, Dilana, how are you?" He was a cutie, there was no doubt about that, and she knew why Rachael found him to be one of her favorites along with his pal, Sadie.

"All the better for coming home, Sam. Where is Sadie?"

The boy grinned wickedly, as he pointed toward the hedge.

Turning in the direction of the finger, Di was about to shout for the girl to come out and say hello when she noticed the figure at the end of the drive. Her heart began to beat rapidly in her chest, her breath shallow. There was no mistaking who it was. Rachael. Di took a tentative step toward the woman she had been aching to see for weeks and who was within reach—

"Dilana, we have an appointment." Her lawyer, Malcolm Randal laid a hand on her arm.

The gesture took her by surprise. She swung around and flashed the man an angry look. He recoiled slightly, immediately removing his hand from her arm while his eyes looked quizzical. "We have an appointment, Dilana."

"I'm sorry, Malcolm. You are right. We have an appointment." Her eyes strayed back to the place where her heart longed to be. Rachael had now gone, and Di could feel bitter disappointment fill her. *Do I want to see her so bad that it was a figment of my imagination?*

"Let's go." Malcolm walked toward the doorway and spoke a few words to the driver.

"Okay, be right with you." Bending down, Di came on level with Sam and his mischievous features. "Sam, I need you to do something for me, if you would?"

"Yeah, sure I will, Dilana."

"Will you ask Rachael if she will meet me in the garden after the meeting with Sister Angela?"

Sam gave the comment serious thought, or as serious as a boy of that age could. Di held a silent breath, waiting for the boy's answer.

"Okay. Can we have another BBQ at the beach soon?"

The mercenary thought processes of the child weren't lost on Di, and she laughed outright at his request. "I'll see what I can do. I need to go. Please, don't forget to ask Rachael for me." She turned, leaving the boy to watch her back as she strode off after the lawyer and entered the building.

✝

Sister Angela's eyes glowered with pent up frustration when she saw Dilana Sterling. Why didn't the bishop tell her that there would be more than a lawyer visiting?

"I'm sorry," she curtly said. "I was only told that we were being visited by a lawyer. Ms. Sterling's appearance is most—unexpected." She held out her hand and shook each one.

"Oh, Bishop Clarence didn't know. I made the original arrangements last month and, as you know, I had to cancel on short notice due to a court date I needed to attend. By the time the new date was agreed upon, Ms. Sterling was back in town. I thought it would be prudent that she attend, since this involves her too." The lawyer smiled in a friendly professional manner and sat down in the chair indicated.

"Yes, I heard she had returned." Sister Angela glanced directly at Dilana and gave her a glare. "Please sit, Ms. Sterling," Sister Angela motioned toward the chair furthest from the desk. A silence filled the room for a few minutes, as neither party attempted to talk. Sister Angela mentally shook her head at the tension building in the room. "Perhaps you could clarify why you are here. As I mentioned before, the bishop was rather sketchy with the facts."

Pulling open his briefcase, Malcolm Randal removed a sheaf of papers and handed over a copy to her. "The reason we are here under such an element of secrecy, Sister, I am sure you will understand once you read the details of the papers in your hand. One which, under the circumstances, you may well approve."

Sister Angela looked at the thick packet of paper and raised an eyebrow. "Thank you, Mr. Randal. I will read them as quickly as possible. Would you care for coffee, tea, or any other type of beverage?"

"Thank you. I'll have coffee, black. Di, do you want anything?"

No response

"Di?" he gently prodded again.

"I'm sorry…water…iced water please."

Sister Angela picked up the phone and pressed the internal button. "Please bring in coffee and ice water." She looked at the two visitors. "Excuse me while I read this. Your drinks should be here momentarily." She placed her spectacles on her nose and began reading.

Malcolm passed a copy to Di. "I thought you might want to see the finished copy."

"Thanks." Dilana began to peruse the document.

There was a faint knock on the door, and a short nun with a ready smile brought in a tray with drinks and cookies.

"Thank you, Sister." As Sister Angela read, she knew her facial expressions went from interest, puzzlement, and finally to surprise. Removing the specs, she clasped her hands together over the document in quiet contemplation and gave the two people her full attention.

"Is there anything you don't understand, Sister?"

"Nothing. Everything. Why have you done this, Ms. Sterling?" She stared at the writer. *This was like the answer to her and the other nuns' prayers.*

"You deserve it." Dilana's cheeks colored. She looked away only to quickly look back to Sister Angela.

"That isn't a proper answer. Please, tell me. Why have you done this?"

Dilana stood and walked over to the window overlooking the garden. Was she looking for someone in particular? "I owed it to you. It's as simple as that." She turned to face the sister.

119

"You owe us nothing. We gave freely, Dilana. I do believe you have equally been generous when you lived here, isn't that so?" Sister Angela watched the writer's face. Strained was the word that came to mind.

"I—I gave the odd BBQ, Sister. It's not quite the same."

"You brought happiness and joy to many with your gesture. We have all reaped the reward, including many who would have otherwise been poorer for the experience. If this is about payment, you had no debt to fulfill and never would have to anyone here."

"Are you sure you speak for everyone?" Dilana asked with a bleak expression.

It would have been easy to misunderstand the question and answer yes. However, Sister Angela knew, just as she suspected the writer did, that this wasn't about the orphans in general. It was about only one orphan. "I think you should ask that question to the party involved, Dilana."

Malcolm, clearing his throat, brought the attention back to the matter at hand. "Ladies, I hope you don't mind, but I wonder if there is anything I can do to clarify the situation here."

"Maybe, Malcolm. Sister do you accept this gift?"

Sister Angela stared at the papers in front of her. Dilana had generously gifted ninety percent of her profits from the book *When Dreams Need the Hand of Faith* to the orphanage. With all the jumbled thoughts Sister Angela had about the author, there was one string attached and it broke her heart. She read the stipulation again. *The Diocese will allow Sister Angela and the current members of the order to remain as custodians of the orphanage until they choose to move on to other projects.*

†

"Rachael, Rachael, will you let me in please? I have a message." Sam bounced up and down outside the teacher's room. Sadie had followed, telling him she wanted to help if she could.

No sound came from inside. "She isn't here." Sam frowned. "I was only a minute behind her."

"Where else would she go?" Sadie asked.

"Come on, Rach, its important," the boy pleaded through the door. To Sam, it was important if they could have their BBQ's and stuff back again on the beach. Everyone had been sad when they ended abruptly. It wasn't enough that they were orphans, but someone had been kind and then removed the gift as quickly as it came. They'd all been angry with Dilana but more so because it had upset Rachael who was their friend. He didn't want to think what it would be like if Sadie moved away and he lost her as a friend. He was going to make sure that Rachael knew her friend was back.

"Maybe she's still mad with her for leaving?" Sadie piped up.

"Don't be silly, Sadie. It was weeks ago and people forget. Look at us. I lost my tooth trying to protect you from those bullies at school and what happened? You were bullying them."

"I was not. They were pulling my pigtails. I didn't like it and let them know it."

"Yeah well, you could have told me first that you had it under control before I ended up with this." He pointed to the gap to the left side of his mouth. Sister Angela had been annoyed but it hadn't lasted much longer than a couple of minutes. After that she was making the appointment for him to see the dentist.

"I think it's a good war wound anyway. Maybe Rachael will do the same to Dilana. Hey, wouldn't that be fun to see?"

"No. No, she can't do that. We might not get our trips to her beach again. You are silly, Sadie." Turning his attention to the closed door, he hammered on the panel and shouted again. "Rachael, it's important. Open the door."

The door cracked open, and Rachael looked out at him. He could see that she had been crying as there were streaks down her cheeks. "Why are you crying, Rachael? Has someone been bullying you? I'll take care of it if they have." Sam puffed out his chest.

Rachael signed to him that, no, she wasn't being bullied and thanked him for his concern.

"Rach, she's here, she's come back to us. Will you meet her in the garden after her meeting with Sister Angela? She asked nicely."

Rachael sucked in a sharp breath before signing. Sam, I'm sorry I have a headache. Tell her another time, perhaps.

"But, Rach, she asked real nice and it won't take a minute." The boy was distressed. If Rach didn't go, perhaps they wouldn't get back the beach BBQ's and stuff.

She may have asked nice, Sam, but I'm tired. As I said, another time. Will you please tell her that for me? Rachael signed.

Sam hung his head and scuffed his toe against the polished wooden floor. "Okay," he mumbled, as he turned away. Sadie tugged on his arm.

"Tell her. Tell her?"

Rachael placed an arm on Sadie's shoulder before her fingers signed, *You tell me, Sadie.*

The girl blushed. Taking hold of Sam's hand, she spoke clearly. "Sam asked Dilana if we could have another BBQ. She said she would see what she could do. We know if you don't go to see her she probably will leave again." The last few words were said in a defiant tone, as Sadie stood hand in hand with Sam.

Fingers quickly said, You think that if I don't see Dilana today, she may not have another BBQ?

"She might not. She likes you, Rachael, maybe she even loves you like we do."

Rachael nodded. I will see her. Go wash up. You look like you've been digging in the garden with your hands.

Sam gave a whoop of joy. With Sadie's hand in his, they headed off down the corridor.

Rachael's smile was bright and warm as she watched them leave.

Oh, if only life was as simple as it had been as a child.

She would see Dilana for the children's sake. Her eyes closed recalling Sam's words that maybe Dilana loved her. *If only that were true.* That was the problem. She now knew that she loved Dilana, and her leaving had hurt so much that she didn't think she could face it all over again. She had nothing to offer Dilana except for her friendship. Apparently, that hadn't been enough for the writer to stay behind the first time. *Why would anything change?* Rachael knew the only way to find out the answer to that question was to meet with Dilana.

✝

"I…I need this point clarified, if you would?" Sister Angela said.

Malcolm Randal inspected the item in question and sat back. "Sister, my client stipulated this was the only requirement she wanted regarding such a generous offer. Although, it's hardly fair to say how generous at this moment. Some works simply don't make the grade, but as you may know, Ms. Sterling's reputation is reasonably solid in producing a highly saleable product. Also, it's number one in many listings. Suffice to say, we expect a reasonable return. That being the case it would, of course, bring a reasonable gift to the orphanage."

Di had to turn back to the window to stop from laughing at the man waffling away. It was so typical of a lawyer who gave out ten words instead of one to describe a situation. To cap it all, he never answered her question either. Would the nun ask again or be intimidated by Malcolm?

"I'm aware of Dilana's reputation, Mr. Randal. We have several of her books here in the library, however, that doesn't answer my question. Did the bishop agree to this stipulation?"

Good for her. Has the sister read my work also?

"I, of course, talked with the bishop prior to the agreement being drawn up. He believed that the book was a potential top seller and could prove very lucrative for the orphanage. He agreed, in principle."

"What does that mean exactly?"

"He decided that you would be the one to agree or not to the stipulation. After all, it is bound to affect you and the rest of the sisters here in the building. Perhaps you need time to talk with them and get back to us?"

"I thought when someone chose to give in this way, there was no contract or agreement or disagreement, the situation was clear. If I choose not to agree to the stipulation, will you remove the offer, Dilana?"

"I believe the contract to be a fair one and really—"

"Leave it, Malcolm. I'll explain. Sister, I wanted you to have as much a share in my success with the book as possible. Nevertheless, I feel that this establishment would be the poorer if you—or any of the current nuns—are removed to other areas, and the place is either closed or passed over to less understanding individuals. That was my only reason for this contract, Sister. If you say to me that I'm wrong to do such a thing and that you do not want this cushion against dramatic change, then I will abide by that and the gift will still remain."

A silence invaded the room once more, but this time, it was of deliberation not animosity.

A quietly spoken voice echoed around the room. "Thank you, Dilana. The gift is most welcome, and though your clause is acknowledged, may I ask that you remove it? It is God's will that keeps us here, and it will be His will that moves our lives along another path, if He sees fit. We cannot be bound by a stipulation in a contract, however well-meaning that clause may be."

Di turned back to face the nun. Her book was number one. The reviews were staggering, and SG said she had already been approached by a producer of a prominent studio who wanted to buy the rights to the book for a movie. The book had only been on the market two weeks. She had great hopes that the generous royalty would eliminate the most immediate financial stresses of the convent and orphanage. It would also enable the nuns to stay there for as long as the book made sufficient funds. She resigned herself to the fact that Sister Angela wouldn't be moved on the subject. She had seen that stubborn stance from the woman before, and

Rachael had said she was an immovable object. "Thank you for reminding me, Sister, that no matter how well-meaning I intended to be, I can't manipulate everyone. Do you think God will forgive me?"

"I will pray for you, Dilana. I'm sure He knows your heart was in the right place."

For a final time, Di turned back to gaze at the place where she was hoping to see Rachael. Maybe God was on her side. Rachael was sitting on the bench under the arch they had shared once before. "Yes, my heart is in the right place." The softly spoken words were barely audible to the others in the room.

"What was that, Di?" Malcolm Randal asked.

"How about you clear up this little matter, Malcolm, and I'll meet you at the car when it's done. Sister Angela, would you excuse me for a short time? There's someone I need to see. I think you understand."

Malcolm's eyebrows rose, and Sister Angela nodded as she quickly crossed the room.

"Yes, we can do that. Would you care for a tour of our little home here, Mr. Randal?"

"Yes, sounds like a good idea to me."

The door to the room opened and shut swiftly, as Dilana sped toward another meeting. One she didn't think would go as easily as this one had, but she had to try and try she would.

✝

Having spent the last ten minutes wondering how long she would have to wait for Dilana, the same thought continued to replay in her mind. Why hadn't her friend told her she was not going to come back for weeks, perhaps ever. *Hadn't they been friends at all?*

"Hi."

A voice she recognized hailed her quietly, dragging her out of her chaotic thoughts. Rachael gazed up into the features of the woman who had caused her to rethink her whole life and undergo a wealth of emotions both wonderful and painful that still didn't entirely make sense to her. Mouthing a hello back, Rachael pointed to the seat beside her which Dilana took.

"Thank you for allowing me some of your time. I know how busy you are, Rachael." The ever faithful notebook was produced, and Rachael began scribbling.

Why did you want to see me, Dilana?

"I owe you an explanation for not coming back sooner."

You owe me nothing. She gave Dilana an intent gaze then continued. *Nothing at all.*

Dilana shook her head. "I do, Rachael, we both know that. It was unforgivable of me to treat a friend in such a way."

Were we friends? I think not in the circumstances. She couldn't look at Dilana and turned away.

"Why do you say that? Of course we were…are. I want us to be friends, Rachael. It is important to me."

Hearing the panic and pain in the writer's tone, Rachael switched around to face the woman. She did not want to inflict hurt on anyone. Especially not on this woman, no matter how aggrieved she felt. *Important now, perhaps. What was it? Was it the book that prompted you to return?*

"Yes, in a way, that's true. The book did prompt my return here in part. The beach house belongs to me now. I was always coming back here. I told you so."

You said it would be a few weeks, at the most, Dilana. Can't you count?

"I deserve your sarcasm, but I want to explain. Are you interested in knowing?"

Rachael caught Dilana's eyes and slowly nodded.

"You might not like what you hear, but you deserve the truth. Please, will you listen to the whole story first, before you make a judgment on me?"

Rachael nodded again. She knew her face was stiff, and inwardly, she wanted to close her ears to an explanation she was sure would hurt her.

"Before I went away, we had a meal at the café near the beach. Remember?"

Rachael nodded. She remembered it all. Every minute of each day she'd spent with the writer. Cherishing them all.

"I lied to you about the second thing I wanted to talk to you about. I said it was about a gift for you, it wasn't." Di glanced down at her tightly clasped hands.

Rachael touched her arm and gave a tentative nod.

"I'm a lesbian, Rachael. I didn't know if you knew that about me then, and I was afraid if you did you wouldn't want us to be friends. When we, well you, were hit on by the women in the bar, I was ashamed of them and how they made many of us appear. I was a coward and decided not to say anything. Now, I wish I'd told you."

Rachael listened intently. She had known about Dilana's preferences in physical relationships. That had never worried her or stopped the intensity of the feeling she had for the writer. On reflection, she wasn't sure if the love she felt for the author was of the physical kind or that of a very good friend without the need to have a physical rapport. However, that didn't detract from the fact that Dilana had lied about more than that in her life. *Hasn't she?*

Go on.

"I had all good intentions of coming home in two weeks. You need to know that it was all worked out that way, and SG had even allowed me to duck some of the publicity events she'd organized. There was one party I went to that caused the problems. I met someone there who made it difficult for me to keep my promise to you."

Rachael kept her features impassive while she listened intently.

Dilana cleared her throat and bit her lip before continuing. "As you now know, I went abroad with her for several weeks. When the new book came out, I came back, and now I'm here to stay. I never intended to hurt you, Rachael. I do want us to be friends, if you can see your way clear to forgive me for not telling you the truth or contacting you about why I stayed away longer."

Are you planning on having your friend live at the beach house too?

"No! Celina and I went our separate ways when I came back to the States. She's no longer a part of my life nor ever will be again. It was a mistake to do what I did, and I'll regret that for the rest of my life. I can promise nothing like that will ever happen again. It's important you understand that." Dilana faced her squarely.

It isn't important to me though. There she had said the words, but as she saw the pain and disbelief cross Dilana's features, she felt a sword pierce her heart. Why had she said that? There wasn't anyone alive more important to her, except perhaps, Sister Angela.

"I accept that. I'm not quite the person that perhaps you thought I was, but I do care for you very much, Rachael. Can you find it in your heart to let me be your friend again? I promise not to screw up this time around."

You can't have cared enough or you would have at least written to me and told me what was happening in your life. I could understand you taking a lover. We were only friends. However, if your idea of friendship is discarding them when a new lover comes on the scene, then no, I'm sorry Dilana, that isn't the kind of friendship I want or deserve.

Dilana reached over to take Rachael's hand and she shoved it away. "Rachael, please, please, don't shut me out. I need to explain that Celina and I..."

Rachael held up a hand and shook her head. *I don't want to hear it.*

"Please, allow me to prove myself to you as a friend. I guarantee you will never see me falter again. Please?"

I did care about you once, Dilana, but not now. You have proved yourself a very poor friend to me and the people here who brought you into their lives. Now, I'm going. Please, don't contact me again. Rachael stood and, without a backward glance, left the garden and moments later entered the orphanage.

Di's legs were lead weights, immovable, as Rachael strode off and disappeared behind a small, wooden door into one of the many annexes of the building.

Finally, her body allowed her to stand. She needed to make sense of her world, as it was spiraling out of control. Had she been a poor friend to everyone? *Everyone?*

The notebook dropped lifelessly from her fingers, as she walked unsteadily toward the archway that would lead her back to the car. Inside, she would take refuge with her pain and wait for Malcolm. Once home, she would cry for all that she had thrown away, because of her own misguided and pigheaded notions that only she could save the day.

Malcolm got in the car and saw his client and friend deeply preoccupied. She had been since they arrived at the orphanage, but now it seemed more pronounced. He wondered if it had anything to do with her hasty retreat from Sister Angela's office.

He had known her for years, having worked with her father in the last ten years of his life. Malcolm had been a young, rookie, hotshot lawyer, and Randolph Sterling was a dedicated and thorough senior partner of the practice. Strangely enough, they became friends, and Randolph took Malcolm under his wing. He'd helped him out on more than one occasion during the years they'd worked together.

During that time, he'd watched Randolph struggle at times to bring up a teenage daughter who was willful and spoiled but bristling with talent. The closeness of the relationship defied the total opposite natures of father and daughter. When Di landed her first publishing contract, Malcolm was given the task of personal lawyer to her. Though she had her own views, it was clear that Randolph's influence in making sure everything was set out on paper had been instilled in his daughter. When her father died, part of her died with him.

When SG contacted him on Di's behalf to oversee a house deal in a rather obscure, small town, he had been pleased that she was finally coming back to life. Her current books proved that in spades, and his wife said her newest was a sweet, feel-good volume that anyone, young and old alike, could read.

Now, looking at her, he knew something was wrong. "Are you all right? Do you want to talk about it?"

"No, I'm fine. Thank you for asking, Malcolm," Di absently replied.

Chapter Eleven

"Go for it, Mrs. D." Di laughed softly, as she watched Dora Drummond enter her first computer poker session on her own. Over the months, she'd found out that her housekeeper was an avid slot player and tried to convince the woman that using the free net games would be a cheaper option for her.

At first, the older woman had been adamant that the computer was for the young, not her old bones, and wouldn't go near it. However, tactically, Di played a few sessions of online poker as well as other casino games. The sound alone drew the woman's glance over Di's shoulder, when she said she was cleaning. Eventually succumbing, she was now going onto her first session alone.

"I'll be back in an hour, Mrs. D. Good luck, and don't get into any trouble while I'm gone."

"Really, you young people. How can I get into any trouble? I'm only playing fake poker." As she spoke, the computer chimed and Dora became embroiled in a chat with another poker player. She'd engaged, with the screen name AcesFull, in a conversation about mischievous people who came to interrupt other's enjoyment of the game.

Yeah, right, Mrs. D, no trouble. Di smiled as she walked toward the balcony steps for a run on the beach. It was a beautiful, sunny afternoon. The heat was tolerable, and she enjoyed stretching her muscles. It made her feel alive.

Life wasn't the best. How could it be? Rachael wasn't part of it any more. Rachael had meant what she said, and they hadn't seen each other since that day in the garden at the orphanage, three months earlier. Fortunately, she was in contact with Sister Angela and had news of Rachael on a regular basis. At least she knew Rachael was well in the world, even though physical contact was now out of the question.

The book was a bonus all around. The orphanage had a good income from sales that still staggered both her and SG. Her publisher's wedding was rescheduled for two weeks hence. Things looked okay for the future, too, as a movie was now a possibility. Malcolm Randal and SG were haggling over terms with the producer. Eventually, they would work something out. Although Di had indicated that she might never write again, the muse bugged her constantly, and no amount of battling it down had been any use. She was writing a children's story, something she never in the world would have thought possible.

Generally, the town had accepted her back into the fold. They congratulated her on the book and when they found out what she had given to the orphanage, they were more than impressed. Any sour grapes over her use of the town and people in the book were now in the past. Even to the point where she had arranged to fund a summer vacation for the orphans, at a camp in Texas. Di was thinking of going too. She'd never ridden a horse in her life, and this was a working ranch designed for children. *Hey, I could be a kid again.* It didn't take much. She chuckled at the thought, as she increased the tempo of her run along the beach.

At this time of day, there weren't many people around. She did several circuits on her private stretch then proceeded along to the public beach, where she ran to the two-mile point and turned back. The exercise was great for her, and she had never felt fitter, body wise, in her life. Her heart was another story. It was aching incessantly for something that she could never attain. It wasn't every day you found the love of your life and discarded it without careful thought. Nowadays, she filled her time writing, running, and more writing. On the weekends, she visited the beach café to spend a few hours playing pool with the owner, and having a few beers along with a meal. It was her concession to SG that she didn't wall herself up in the beach house as she had in her apartment after her father's death.

Once the weather warmed up more, she would reinstate the monthly BBQ's for the orphanage. Bob Drummond and his merry band had willingly agreed to help as they had the summer before. All was well on that front. She didn't quite know how she would feel when Rachael didn't show on those Saturdays but, as with everything, time and getting on with things would help. She wasn't going to deprive the children of this treat because she had screwed up and lost a dear friend in its wake.

No amount of teasing by Sister Angela would persuade her to go back to church, though she had made an exception at the Christmas carol singing, shortly after she'd arrived back. It was a wonderful feeling to be part of that event, and she was sure it had been the nail that sealed the coffin lid on her staying in Meredith permanently. There was a time, after Rachael's rejection, when she had wavered about going back to the city. Now, she knew that the beach house was where she belonged.

As she settled into a jog a few hundred yards from her beach area, she saw a figure standing and looking out over the sea to the horizon. Her heart rate tripled. She tried and failed to see who it was, damn she should have put her contacts in.

Increasing the pace of her run, she swiftly came up to the silent person. Although it would be impossible not to hear her feet pounding on the sands, the figure hadn't turned to look in her direction.

As Di came closer she said, "Hi, can I help you?"

The person in question turned around. Di gasped. How could she have forgotten so easily?

"Hi, Di, are you pleased to see me?" Celina Ratford smiled warmly, while her eyes appreciatively roamed over Di's body.

"I'm surprised to see you, Celina. What brings you here?" Di feigned politeness when she wanted to be angry.

"I figured that as you hadn't returned to town for any of the parties that SG has given on your behalf, I would come this way and seek you out. I also wanted to find out what's so special about this place that made you abandon your friends in the city."

"Other than SG, I haven't any friends in the city. I thought you knew that." A look, reminiscent of a sharp, short pain, crossed the older woman's features at the remark.

"I'm your friend, Dilana. I thought we had at least established that in our relationship?"

"You may have, Celina. I, on the other hand, haven't come to that conclusion. What we had together—I doubt that is the right word since we never were together—is over. It was an…interlude in both our lives that is best forgotten."

Celina moved closer.

"Forgotten, Di? I'll never forget you, and I don't think you can forget me either. It wasn't all one sided. I think, no, I know we had good times together. Remember that party, the meal we had in that beachside restaurant in Turkey? We watched the sun go down, and you confided in me that it was great for your muse. I'd call that together."

Di closed her eyes briefly. She was unable to deny that Celina was good company, as long as she wasn't trying to get her in bed. They had indeed spent many hours in the early evenings enjoying the sunsets. Conversations with Celina had been entertaining and knowledgeable. The plain truth was that Di's heart was given, and there was nothing Celina could do to change that. If she and Rachael never talked again, it would be enough for Di to know that she was having a good life, even if it didn't include her.

"Why are you here, Celina? To bring up old times that are best forgotten? I don't want to go down memory lane with you. We both had a good time, but it was never going to be the great romance you wanted. I think you need to leave, and this time, please don't come back."

"Are you throwing me out of town?"

"I'm asking you nicely to leave. If you want me to throw you out, I will. Trust me, I'm capable."

"Would you have one coffee with me for old times? Then I promise to go and never come back here again."

Di shook her head. "I'd rather not, Celina. I'm running, and I don't want to break my pattern."

"Your housekeeper said you were due back. Did you know she uses your computer to play games when you are out?"

Di shook her head at the petty remark. *How like Celina to point that out.* "How the hell do you know that? Did you go inside my house?"

Cleina rolled her eyes. "No, the woman was agitated that she'd lose her turn on a game."

"For the record, not that I have to explain anything to you, I set her up before I came out for the run." Di smirked.

A look of peevishness settled on Celina's face. "Is she here with you?"

Astonished at the question and wondering what she meant, Di looked at her quizzically with one eyebrow raising in reaction. "She? Who is she?"

"Don't give me that innocent *I don't know what you're talking about*, Di. She, as in Rachael. That's why you want me out of here, isn't it? Your lover wouldn't approve of me?"

Bristling anger overcame Di, as Celina talked about Rachael. The small space between them became minute. Di shot a hand out and painfully held onto Celina's bony shoulder. "Never, ever, speak of Rachael in that way again, Celina, or I'll do more than bruise your skinny collarbone. I'll break your neck," she growled in a low, threatening tone.

"Does she know you use violence to make a point?"

"You know nothing about her, or me, Celina. You never did. Get off my property, now." Di watched her pout. Celina, as always, never gave up easily.

"You wrote your last book for her, didn't you? I've read the inscription. All the time you were with me you were in love with her. How does she feel about you now, Dilana? You left her to travel with me. Have you managed to explain our relationship, or is she so mercenary she doesn't care how you get a book to sell?"

Di closed her eyes trying to rein in her temper. She wanted to strangle the woman. However, some of what she said was true.

"I wrote the book for the orphanage run by the nuns, and I stay here because I love it here. Why would I want to go back to the city if predators and users like you infest the streets? For the record, again, Rachael is a friend not a lover. I'm sure this bit of information will make you happy—she doesn't want anything to do with me, because I lied to her when I went away with you." The only way she knew to vent her fury was by spitting out her anger with words rather than doing so physically.

Di caught Celina's gaze, and she narrowed hers waiting for a response. Celina laughed a brittle laugh that Di remembered so well, because it used to irritate her to no end. "What are you laughing at? Can't you just leave?"

"I think the situation is so ironic. I do believe you may have fallen for a nun, Dilana. Knowing you can't have her, you've decided that no one can have you. I did wonder when you wrote that dedication, it was so—spiritual."

What am I doing here sparring with this woman? I didn't like her from the first moment I met her. The circumstances of close familiarity had only increased the feeling, which had tempered with absence. Now, it came flooding back, like the lock gates being opened, and she wanted nothing more than to see the woman out of her life and torn out of her memories.

"I don't care what you think, Celina. I never will. Now, this is your exit stage right, or in this case, out of the side entrance under the house. I'll see you out personally. How's that for hospitality?" Di turned toward the house and the place she'd indicated. Slowly, Celina made her way to where Di was standing and gave her a mixed look of anger and hopelessness. "I know you might not believe me, Dilana, but all I want is your happiness." Her shoulders slumped.

Di showed her the exit in silence with a grim expression creasing her features. Closing and locking the side door behind the woman, Di leaned against it and shut her eyes. Had she finally lain to rest the ghost of Celina, or was that a flavor of the haunting yet to come? A heavy sigh escaped her as she trudged back up the stairs to the house and tried to put on a smile for her housekeeper. If she allowed Mrs. D to see her looking glum she would want to know everything and if she didn't get to know, she'd make it up and that wouldn't help Di's life in Meredith at all.

†

Earlier that day...

"Are you ready, Sadie?"

Sadie flipped her pigtails bouncing at the back of her neck, nodding as she picked up her small back pack. "Yep. Did you bring your food too?"

"Yeah, of course. We need our lunch. It's part of the adventure, silly."

Sam grinned and waited for Sadie to catch up to him. They had been planning this adventure for some time now, and today the weather was just dandy and everything should be okay. No one would miss them. It was Sister Josie's turn to watch out for them, and she was almost blind. Anyway, they would be home by dinner full of daring deeds to tell the others, especially that Frankie who thought they constantly told lies. Still, as an eleven-year-old, he had no sense of adventure and anyway, he was getting too old.

"I think it's a great adventure don't you, Sam? We might become famous like those boys and girls in the book Sister Christina reads to us at bedtime." Sadie grinned.

"Oh, Sadie, you're silly. They aren't famous. The books are called *The Famous Five*." He chuckled. What they could do with was a dog, like in *The Famous Five*. But, they would have to do with taking Ben. He was a dog, but a toy and well loved. It was the only thing that Sam had from his birth parents.

"Well, I think they're famous." Sadie pouted and strode by him, down the flight of stairs and out into the early morning sunshine. *Yep, today was a good day for an adventure.*

†

"Rachael, may I talk with you?" Sister Angela moved to the left of the sofa to allow her to sit. Rachel indicated she'd use sign language to converse.

"I don't want to pry, Rachael, and I know you have your reasons, but will you reconsider seeing Dilana Sterling? She asks about you every time we speak, and I know she really was sorry for any pain she caused you."

No.

"No? That's it, end of conversation?" Sister Angela was stunned at the response. Rachael wasn't one to bear a grudge, but she appeared to have changed and have one against the writer. If only the child would confide in her.

We talked and found we didn't have as much in common as we originally thought.

Sister Angela shook her head. "I see. You once told me that you loved her, Rachael. Has that love died too?" A look of pain flashed into the expressive, azure eyes.

140

No, my love is still there, but it exists for someone who isn't real.

"Want to tell me what the reality is? Sometimes, a burden shared is a burden halved."

I don't understand how she could treat our friendship so lightly and simply leave without at least telling me why. She was my friend, and all I wanted was to be her friend. She just left me.

Sister Angela felt the raw emotion that Rachael was feeling from her expressions and the speed of her hand signals. The child was in a torment that Sister Angela hadn't understood, and although she was pleased nothing sexual had happened between the writer and Rachael, it was clear that this was the crux of the problem. "Is that all?"

Is that all? Sister, she left me. She told me she was a lesbian and that she had gone away with another woman. I think that's enough, don't you?

Sister Angela smiled gently and tenderly placed a hand on Rachael's to stop the agitation. "There is a solution to all this, Rachael. It's very simple."

Large eyes peered at her.

What's that, Sister?

"You can confront Dilana with your feelings and discuss the matter. Even shout and get angry if that will make you feel better. I know she doesn't realize the extent of your pain, and if she did then perhaps you can come to some agreement."

What kind of agreement? Isn't not seeing her enough?

"Yes, it is for you, at the moment. What about the other orphans? They won't understand when you refuse to go to the monthly BBQ's and she refuses to come here for dinner as she used to, because she's promised not to see you.

Sam and Sadie have already commented that they don't understand why you never see her like you did. They say you are always sad."

I'm not always sad—am I?

"Sometimes, my dear. We all want to help, but I don't think anyone can. Only you and perhaps Dilana can. Maybe the solution is for her to go away again, but this time for good."

No. She can't go away again. She can't.

There was no doubt about that reaction. Sister Angela smiled. "If she makes you miserable all the time, I think she will want to do that and then you might be happier. Unless you want her to suffer, too, for your pain and keep her at arm's length for the rest of your lives."

Sister, what do I do? I feel so unhappy. I know deep down that Dilana isn't a liar as I called her. If I go to see her do you think she'll forgive me and we might try to be friends again?

Encasing the child in a tender hug she kissed the top of the chestnut hair and smiled "I think she will gladly try again, child. It's close to dinner, why not go over and invite her. Call it the ice breaker and then see from there."

Grinning, Rachael hugged her before leaving with a skip in her step that hadn't been seen since last year.

Sister Angela watched Rachael leave, her heart feeling that much lighter. Perhaps the road for the two of them might be rocky, and they might never achieve the level of happiness they once had in each other's company. In the end, you take the rough with the smooth. Love had a way of handling that in its own way.

She frowned as she realized that she could have sent Rachael down a path that the bishop wouldn't approve. Standing and breathing in deeply, she went toward the door on her way to check on Sister Christina and her charges. Her last thought on that subject… *What the bishop doesn't know can't hurt anyone.*

✝

Sam placed a hand on his chin, and Sadie watched him. She thought he looked quite grown up as he looked over the raft they had built over the winter. They had stored it in a small cave, close to the shore, and were now ready to take it on a journey that they had only dreamed about. They had first decided on the idea when Rachael told them a story about pirates and treasure islands and someone called Robinson Crusoe. After that, they agreed that the sea was the place for them to experience adventurers like in the books.

Sam had come across the twigs and sticks that represented most of the raft they'd built, after farmer Pool had cut down some of his old trees. They acquired twine and thread from various sources, but generally the nun's sewing baskets when they weren't looking. Sister Agatha's garden shed had been a mine of useful items to help them with their project.

Proudly puffing out his chest, Sam exclaimed, "I think we are ready, Sadie. It looks great!"

Glancing at Sam and then at the object that he enthused about, she had to agree. The raft was a work of art, and they had built it together. It might look a little wonky, but it would be as Sam said, great, just like in the books.

"Yeah, it is, Sam. What do we do now?"

"We push it into that inlet over there." He pointed to a small inlet that was hidden from view of the villas on the beach.

"Will it have a strong enough tide to take us out to sea?"

"Yeah, of course it will. I've been watching it for months."

"When? You never told me." Sadie pouted her disapproval at being left out of the appraisal.

"Every time we had a BBQ here. You were too busy eating."

Affronted, Sadie exaggerated her pout and stamped her foot. "I was not. How can you say that, Sam Campbell?"

Sam grinned. "You are just so easy to rile. Okay, I got it wrong. Now come on, Sadie, we need to launch. Don't the adults usually have a celebration like smashing a bottle of wine or something?"

"We haven't any wine, Sam—hey maybe this will do." She rummaged in her bag and found a plastic bottle that held her soda.

"You are wonderful, Sadie. It's just the ticket."

The praise made Sadie blush slightly, as she reveled in getting something right. Sam Campbell could be a hard act to follow when he was on a roll.

The boy grasped the bottle from Sadie and grinned. "Now you need to say something, Sadie, as I swing the bottle."

"I do? Oh, okay. I name this raft—what shall I name it, Sam?"

"Anything you want, silly."

"Oh, okay. I name this raft, Rachael." Sadie glowed with pride, as Sam gave her a brilliant smile.

"Now let's take her in the water and set off on our journey. You never know, we might discover something, another country, like Columbus used to do." Gleefully, Sam stepped aboard the raft. It sank into the water but then floated upwards as he held out a hand for her.

Once Sadie was aboard, they paddled with both hands toward the mouth of the inlet. This would be one fantastic adventure.

†

"Okay, how many millions of points have you accumulated, Mrs. D?" Di asked. She wearily sank into the sofa opposite the computer where her housekeeper was happily playing net poker.

"Not as many as I would have liked. That piggy certainly doesn't like me. It makes me wait for over an hour before it fills up. How can I seriously get to a million?" The older woman slowly typed a message and the screen changed. She had obviously logged out of the game.

"Addictive though, don't you think? The only thing it costs you is your time." Di smiled, as she removed her shoes and decided that a shower was more appropriate. "I'll go for a shower while you play a little."

"Yes, it is. What will my Bob say when I ask him for a computer for my next birthday? He'll think I've gone mad."

"Nah, he'll think he's married to a groovy chick." Laughing at the comical expression on Dora's face, Di shook her head.

"Really, Dilana. You will be taking me back to my youth with expressions like that." Dora chuckled.

"Good, it doesn't do any harm to be reminded of our old memories from time to time."

"How about a nice cup of coffee after you've had a shower?"

Yep, she was probably ripe, her normal hour of running had extended to over two, and she was ready for the relaxing spray. "I'd love that, thank you. Did you ask Bob about next Saturday and a BBQ for the orphanage?"

"Heck, he was pestering me so much about it, how could I forget?" Dora bustled around the room and then went into the kitchen.

"Pleased to hear it," Di said softly, as she sank back into her sofa. It would be so easy to let the world go by and relax into a nap, but that encounter with Celina had hyped her up and that always helped the creative juices flow. Therefore, a good writing session would help.

Her life was in a good routine, one she enjoyed. Okay, she knew that the biggest enjoyment would be for Rachael to forgive her and accept her as part of her life. However, that wasn't going to happen anytime soon. Rachael had made that clear. Nonetheless, if she worked toward that goal, who knew, the fates might be watching out for her. Maybe, just maybe, they might take pity on her. *Yeah, who am I kidding?* The chances are the fates would mock her and take away the one she loved the most in this world as they had her father. *Damn, why can't you pick out a path in life with certain known facts and live with that instead of all these variables that tapped you on your head. You didn't stand a chance of understanding why or what to do.*

She'd better have that shower or the coffee would tempt her to stay put. Time appeared to disappear so fast these days. "I'm going for a shower, Mrs. D," she shouted out her destination. Just as she opened the door to the hall that led to the bathroom, she heard a terrible scream.

†

Rachael had spent over an hour in her room, trying to pen an appropriate message for Dilana. She had destroyed so many, her wastebasket was overflowing. How could she just go over without at least explaining why she was there and what she wanted? It was probably better for her to make the effort now, when it was fresh in her mind. Besides, Dilana might not be there and she could leave the note then wait to see if Dilana turned up for dinner later that day.

Picking up her pen, she tried again…

Dear Dilana,

Would you like to come to dinner this evening?

Regards, Rachael

Another note hit the wastebasket.

Yeah, that would work, right. What a fool she was. Her friend would want to know that she wasn't going to be subjected to another cold shoulder, which now, was the farthest thing from her mind.

Dear Dilana,

I'm sorry for my attitude of late. Can we start again, please? I want to be friends again. Will you come to dinner this evening at the orphanage?

Best regards,

Your friend, Rachael

Okay that was closer to what she wanted to say. Would it be enough to kick start the friendship? Would Dilana want to start again? She could easily make other friendships. *There are plenty of people out there who would want to be associated with her. After all, isn't that the real reason why I chose to sever the friendship?* Her other *friend*?

Dear Dilana,

I know I've been particularly cold to you lately, and maybe I was hasty and didn't give you a chance to explain the situation properly. Would you accept this olive branch in the form of dinner at the orphanage this evening for us to try again?

> Yours,
> Rachael

That is more like it. She thought it still lacked something, though what it was she didn't know.

Scrunching up another note, she tossed it at the basket. This time, it was one too many as it rocked over with the weight of the paper.

Walking over to pick up her debris, she contemplated the numerous efforts to make peace with the writer. Why didn't she just tell her the truth? Surely that was the simplest way?

Selecting another sheet of paper, she attempted to place what was in her heart on the note. It would be up to Dilana to decide what the next step would be.

An hour later, she left the building and took the short cut toward the beach. It would be so good to see her friend again, even if they didn't make it back to the place they had. With a bounce in her step that had been missing for far too long, she felt that it would all come out right. She was sure Dilana would accept the effort she was making, and all that she hoped now was that the writer hadn't forgotten her and moved on with her life.

Sister Angela's admission that Dilana still asked after her made her smile. Everything would be okay. She knew it. Just as she had known that her friend could be an important part of her life until she took her last breath.

It was a beautiful day except for a cooling breeze that whipped her hair around her shoulders. She tied it back from becoming tangled up and giving her the wild look. As she neared the beach, she could smell the freshness of the ocean and all it meant to her, despite her tragic experiences with this natural wonder. It was becoming a far happier experience for her after meeting Dilana. They had both wandered aimlessly, looking for someone, or something, to give their lives that extra meaning. It made you want to celebrate every morning you woke up, because things were good in your life.

As she slipped her shoes off and felt the coolness of the sand underfoot, she made her way leisurely toward the beach house of her friend. Her heart was thumping away inside her chest in an erratic way. She was full of excitement and trepidation, all at the same moment. The only important thing on her mind—she loved Dilana Sterling. They would work out what that love meant and how it would affect their relationship. Smiling, she looked down at the note clutched in her left hand that explained everything. Why she had been so hurt and wanted to lash out at the writer for her inability to see how important she had become in her life. She thought her friend had felt the connection as well.

As she neared the stretch of beach she called her own, she heard faint cries and was unable to see where they came from at first. It might just be the gulls acknowledging she had returned home. She always felt an affinity with the wild birds, just as she did the ocean itself.

Turning her gaze toward the horizon, she saw something unfamiliar bobbing up and down. She squinted at the object, which was being buffeted viciously on the waves. Whatever it was, it looked innocuous from this distance, but Rachael knew that up close it probably wasn't. *What is it?*

Straining to see more, she heard the cries again. She realized that there must be someone in trouble out on the waves. Didn't they know that this time of the year was dangerous to go out any farther than wading distance? The waves in this area could be cruel, and she would know. Wouldn't she?

Nearing the edge of the shore, she felt the ocean at her feet, tickling her toes and tempting her to follow it's lapping in and out of the beach. How could she communicate with the people? She could tell that the object wasn't a boat. It didn't look like more than a few pieces of wood. It was hardly serviceable for taking out into sea.

Turning, her eyes searched the area only to realize that her only choice was to run to Dilana's beach house and hope that someone was home and they could help. As she began running, she heard a frightened voice shout what sounded like her name. Rachael stopped and listened. She was sure it was her name but didn't know how whoever it was would know it was her. Glancing back, her resolve to go for help wavered with her need to assist the unfortunate victims of this potential tragedy.

"Rachael! Rachael! Please help us!"

There it was again, and this time she had no hesitation. She dropped her shoes and the note onto the sandy beach and stripped off her jacket and dress allowing her the freedom to swim out without encumbrance. *God help me*, she prayed, as she dove into the cold water. Barely recognizing the cold, with all her strength, she swam as fast as she could toward the object and its frightened occupants.

†

"Mrs. D? What's the matter? Has something happened?" Di ran toward the kitchen where she had heard the housekeeper's scream. It was probably another of those large spiders the woman hated.

As she neared Dora, she saw the housekeeper's body trembling while wildly pointing out the window that faced the ocean.

"What are you looking—what the hell?"

"She just stripped off her clothes and jumped in, Dilana. I can't see why!" the woman remarked.

All Di could see was a swimmer heading toward a few pieces of driftwood in the distance.

"Who did, Mrs. D?"

"Rachael," Dora screamed.

Di stared hard, as the woman she loved swam out toward what appeared to be driftwood but—no—there was something else. "Mrs. D, call the police or the fire department...whoever it is that does rescue. We have a situation. There are people out there in trouble." Di rushed toward the door, thankful she wasn't wearing her sneakers so she wouldn't have to waste time kicking them off.

"Where are you going?" Mrs. D screamed.

"To help of course. Rachael needs me." The words were merely an echo, as Di shot off and sped down the stairs at the side of the house and down to the beach.

For a moment, Mrs. D watched, helpless, as she saw the writer sprinting as fast as she could toward the spot where Rachael had gone into the ocean. She shook her head, and wasting no more time, called the authorities for emergency help.

†

Rachael swam as fast as she had ever done in her life. She had been taught to swim from an early age. Her parents were avid sailors and thought it a natural extension of her education. They had even commented, just before they died, that she was stronger than either of them. A fact that was proven when freak waves washed over their small vessel and threatened to break it apart. The waves that came out of nowhere became dangerously aggressive. It took her parents' expertise to keep them afloat, but one wave too many had finally washed them all overboard. Rachael had no recollection of the events during that time. Perhaps, it was because she refused to acknowledge the traumatic event. All she remembered was swimming to a life ring and grasping it desperately. As suddenly as the waves had reached high, the ocean became tranquil. She looked around and found that she was alone.

Was she now going to experience the same thing again? Would she have to endure watching others fight Poseidon himself for their lives? *No.* The simple demand echoed in her head, determinedly. She would ensure that the same fate was not meted out to these unfortunates, however foolish they had been. Swimming closer, she tried to see who was calling her name. The crashing waves, not to mention the wind's increasing power, made it difficult to see. The spray from the churning water hit her full on the face, but she continued her battle with the ferocious waves.

Rachael grasped a piece of the wood that almost knocked her out. When she hauled herself up to see who the victims were, her mouth opened and subsequently filled with salt water. Coughing, she spit it out and stared in shock. Sam Campbell and Sadie Thompson were clinging to one piece of flimsy wooden board looking terrified. Another wave engulfed them, and Rachael cried inside as both children screamed in fear.

Damn it, how am I going to communicate? Signing was out of the question since she needed both hands to keep afloat.

Another wave crashed over them, and the children wailed in fright. Rachael could see tears of helplessness run down their cheeks mingling with the salt water that covered them as each wave descended.

She mouthed *hold on tight and it will all be okay.* She would make it okay. They trusted her to do that, and she'd do everything in her power to make it happen.

Her mind was working out several ways of saving them but none would guarantee success. She was alone, and the children's fear meant they would cling to her like limpets. If they panicked, none of them would survive. She wondered if she would, once again, be unable to prevent a tragedy that was happening before her eyes. This time though, she probably would be one of the causalities.

She saw Sam pointing in the direction of the beach. Had her prayers been answered, had someone else seem them?

"Dilana. It's Dilana. She's coming to help us, Rachael," Sam spluttered before being engulfed by another wave. She heard the crack of wood as it split in half, carrying the two children in opposite directions. With lightning reflexes, she grabbed hold of the firmest piece and caught Sadie before she was swallowed by the wave. The child was crying profusely and thrashing about, unable to stop the panic that overtook her. She flailed her arms and almost took Rachael under. They still had to save Sam who was clinging to a smaller piece of wood and floating farther from her reach. She gave Sadie a bright smile and mouthed, *we will save him I promise.*

Rachael felt, rather than heard, Dilana at her shoulder. It was that feeling of peace and calm that settled within her whenever she was in the company of the writer. Even now, with this chaos around them, Di's presence still managed to work its magic. Fortunately for Rachael, the feeling weaved into the child who stopped thrashing around when the writer grinned at her.

"I'll take her, Rachael."

Rachael nodded and gave a smile, as she placed Sadie in Dilana's strong hold then turned back into the waves.

Di turned her head and a crashing wave engulfed her for a moment. When she came up for air, she saw Rachael battling another ferocious wave.

"Sam, will she save Sam?"

Di looked down at the child clinging to her like a second skin. "Rachael will save Sam, Sadie. She's a good swimmer. I promise." It was the truth.

Rachael was a good swimmer. Di had found that out when she had foolishly challenged Rachael to a swim last summer and been well and truly beaten. It had been a fun day, and Rachael was the best by a long way. A small package with a powerful punch. *You'd better still be in shape, Rachael.* Di desperately wanted to stay in Rachael's vicinity, but she had Sadie to think about and began to swim slowly back to the beach with her precious cargo.

Rachael saw her target and swam like a bat out of hell. In the distance, she saw a wave that looked to be far greater in magnitude than the previous ones. Sam would be the first hit, and he wasn't likely to survive something so ferocious. Increasing her pace, she miraculously grasped Sam's collar seconds before the wave crashed over them. As they went under, she felt the rush of water entering her nose, ears, and mouth. Memories invaded her...

Her dad was floating under the water, but he wasn't like her dad. His eyes were staring at her, and he wasn't smiling. He always smiled. She reached out, and her hand was grasped and pulled away.

She gasped for breath as the air hit her, and she turned to the person who had dragged her back.

"Mom."

Her mother smiled. "Poppet, remember what we taught you."

Rachael nodded, as her mother smiled then disappeared as a gigantic wave crashed over them and severed their tentative hold.

Not happening again on my watch. She increased the pressure on Sam's body and held on, hoping and praying that this time it would be different. They came up, gasping for breath, and she pulled Sam closer. She didn't miss the terrified expression on his face. *Is he breathing? It isn't going to end this way. I won't let it.*

Her mouth opened to shout out to the sea that it couldn't have Sam. "You can't have him he is mine." A vaguely familiar voice resonated in her ears. *Was that my voice?*

"Sam? Come on Sam, wake up." *It was her voice.* She had finally broken through the silent barrier that tragedy had created all those years ago when her parents died.

"Sam, I need you awake, come on, please, for me?" She coughed as she gulped in an unwelcome mouthful of the ocean.

The boy blearily opened his eyes. and although his chin wobbled as the tears drifted down his cheeks, he managed a weak smile. She realized that he was far too tired from the ordeal to say anything.

"We're going home, Sam. Hold on to me, tight."

With the boy held close to her, Rachael turned and headed back to shore, constantly dredging into her reserves of energy. She realized that Sam was little more than dead weight holding on to her like a leech. Each stroke was harder and harder to make, and she felt like she had been in the water for hours when it could hardly have been more than ten minutes.

Just as she felt her energy levels sagging, the weight of the boy was taken from her. She looked up from her concentrated view of her destination to smile into the warm grey eyes of the love of her life. Now the phrase, "a sight for sore eyes," fit the bill exactly.

"I'll take him, Rachael. We're nearly there." Di pointed toward the shore, where Sadie was being huddled in a blanket by Mrs. D.

"Great, thanks." Rachael would have laughed if she could at the shock and surprise that crossed the writer's face.

"You spoke?" Dilana's voice was a pitch higher.

"Yes."

Di grinned and turned to begin the journey back to the beach.

Sam blinked at them both and pointed toward a very small object bobbing a few feet away. A large wave threatened to take it out to sea "Ben. We've left Ben," he cried.

Rachael heard the boy's cry, but she didn't remember seeing anyone else. *Is there someone else in danger?* Turning back, she saw the object. Her mind deliberated over the situation for just a few seconds before she made her decision and turned back to the shore.

Chapter Twelve

Di held Rachael close as they sat together on a multicolored blanket on their private stretch of beach. The sun was beginning to set, soon it would be dark. Darkness wasn't something that described her life these days. Sunny prospects filled each day for one reason alone—the woman held close to her breast. Rachael was her life's breath. Di's existence had been rejuvenated from the first day she'd seen her standing on the beach.

"Why so quiet?"

"Just contemplating, my love." Di smiled and kissed the top of Rachael's head.

Rachael turned in her hold and looked deep into Di's eyes and grinned. "Dare I ask what you are contemplating?"

Chuckling, Di hugged her tight and kissed the lips that now allowed sound to pass through them. As they withdrew, Di could see excitement and frustration mirrored in Rachael's eyes. "Nothing nefarious if you wondered."

"I didn't think that." Rachael sighed. "Dilana?"

"Yes?" Di smiled.

"I was thinking—"

"Dangerous, my love." Di winked and heard her love give a soft snort. "Sorry, what do you need to know?"

"We've been together for four months now, and don't get me wrong, I think it's wonderful but—we never get past the kissing stage and…"

Di frowned when Rachael stopped speaking.

Rachael removed herself from Di's hold, stood, and walked a few paces to the gently lapping ocean.

"Rachael, I'm sorry, I don't understand the question? Aren't you happy?" Di got up and walked to stand beside her love. "Tell me what you want, and I promise if it's in my power, I will work hard to get it for you."

Rachael half turned, gave Di a slight smile and held up her hands. "If you don't know what I want, then perhaps this is all wrong."

The quietly spoken words surrounded Di like a wind tunnel. She had made so many mistakes in the past, but she thought that the way she was doing things now was on the up and up. What had she done wrong other than take their relationship slow, ok more like pedestrian.

"You can't even answer me. I knew it! You just want to be friends. You probably think I'm too innocent to know what a lesbian relationship entails. You'd be wrong. I think it's time I went home."

The last words resonated unhappily in Di's brain, as she watched Rachael wrap her arms protectively around her stomach. Rachael didn't seem inclined to go home as she'd said. That was a good thing. It gave Di a chance to salvage this stupid misunderstanding. If only Rachael knew how many times she'd masturbated to relieve her sexual tension after Rachael left.

"Rachael, first and foremost, I love you in every way. I thought you knew that. Obviously, I still have to learn more about you, and I do, so very much, want to know every facet of you." Di hesitated and hoped Rachael would respond. She didn't. Her eyes remained locked on the moon taking precedent in the darkening sky. "You are so important to me, I want everything we explore together now to be right for both of us—"

"You don't think I'm right for you, do you? Is it that woman?"

Di wanted to laugh, first at the irrationality of the statement and second because there hadn't been another woman in her life since the day she met Rachael. *I thought I explained all that.* "What woman are you talking about?"

Rachael turned to her and scowled. "That woman, Celina. You spent a lot of time with her alone, and before you say it again, I know you *said* nothing happened. Is that true of all your relationships, Dilana? Do you never get to home base? Have you ever truly had a lover?"

SG would have a ball with this conversation, that's for sure. The image of her friend laughing uncontrollably at the way this conversation had gone made her roll her eyes.

Di reached over the short distance between them and took Rachael's hand in hers. "Truth is, I'm frightened of going to home base with you, because I love you so much. You know all about my past from what you've read about me and what I've admitted." She took Rachael's other hand, and they stood before the shore with the ocean getting closer to their feet. "My life is complete with you in it, and to be honest, the only thing I want right now is for you to live your life with me. I figure I have the right place, so that's a plus." Di pointed to her home behind them.

Di's hands were squeezed hard. She looked at Rachael and saw tears running down her cheeks. "I'm sorry, love, if—" Rachael lifted a hand and placed her fingers on her lips. Di kissed the two digits.

Rachael moved nearer, and Di pulled her close and kissed her deeply. When they broke away, they both smiled and Di rested her head on Rachael's forehead. "I love you to distraction. Please, don't leave me ever."

"Never. That's a given. I guess you need to talk to Sister Angela about us living together."

Di grinned. "Guess I better had. Family, right?"

"Right."

Di pulled Rachael close. "I have a beautiful sunset to help with the frustration for a little while longer. Is that ok? Oh, and you in my arms."

"Not perfect, but it is as close as I could ever imagine. I love you, Dilana." Rachael snuggled closer.

"Love you too, my daughter of Poseidon."

✝

"It won't work, Rachael. I'm sorry. How can I allow it?"

"Allow it? I'm a grown woman, and I make my own decisions. This one isn't up for bartering. I want to spend my life with Dilana and she with me. We love each other. How much better can that be?"

Di watched the two women face each other off. Neither wanting to give in and both believing they were right. Rachael's certainty that Sister Angela would rubber stamp their relationship wasn't going so well, much as Di had expected. Rachael, on the other hand, thought it a slam dunk, especially as the nun was her surrogate mother. In Di's

161

experience that never quite happened the way you thought it should.

"You know what this will mean? If you love her, how can you ask her to do this?" Sister Angela turned to Di with eyes sparkling, challenging her to refute her meaning.

Helplessly holding up her hands to the nun, Di wiped a hand over her face trying to come up with a convincing suggestion that would keep both women happy. This stalemate would have only one conclusion—a split would happen in one or the other of Rachael's relationships. She didn't want to see that, in fact it was paramount that Rachael and her surrogate family stay together. If it meant that the close friendship they shared was all that it ever would become, she would make their relationship work, somehow. Hurt like hell, but Rachael was her priority now and forever.

They had talked about this meeting with Sister Angela and how to explain what they wanted their lives to be. They would live together, and Rachael would continue working at the orphanage school. Di would write from the beach house. She would carry on her commitment to the orphanage in any way she could. They would be together. *Perhaps it isn't as easy as we thought.*

"Can we find a solution that isn't so black and white from both of your points of views?" Di offered.

"Dilana, there shouldn't have to be a middle ground. I'm an adult not a child," Rachael's tone was defiant.

"You're acting like a spoiled child at this moment, Rachael," Sister Angela angrily retorted.

Di had been as shocked as the nun seemed to be when Rachael walked into the office the morning after they'd talked. Rachael broke the news to Sister Angela bluntly, telling her that she was going to live with Di as her lover.

That seemed to be the end of story for Rachael. It was obvious from the sister's reaction that the words had hurt her.

"I am not."

Di half expected to see Rachael stomp her foot. She didn't.

"Rather than bringing up the pitfalls, where is the compassion for our situation? Is it because we are two women wanting to have a relationship and the church only acknowledges a man and woman? I thought the church taught love, not bigotry."

The defeated look on Sister Angela's face and the hurt in Rachael's tore at Di's heart. She was the reason for this. Perhaps in hindsight, it might have been good to talk strategy before speaking with Sister Angela. At least now they knew the extent of prejudice they would face from all areas. She had hoped, though, that as this was Rachael's "family," they might be a little more compassionate toward the situation.

"Didn't you think this situation might occur, Sister?" Di asked and watched the nun as several expressions crossed her face. The most telling was guilt. "Don't answer that, Sister, I already know."

The nun stood and turned away from them both. Di looked at Rachael and wondered what to do next. It was then the nun spoke so quietly Di had to strain to hear her words.

"I've expected this, yes. From the first day Rachael spoke of you, Dilana, I knew. She was so animated. When we found out who you were, it was easy to assume that you might influence Rachael."

Di could see that Rachael was about to jump in with a comment, but she stopped her by placing her finger on her lips and shaking her head.

The nun continued uninterrupted. "I didn't say anything. I wanted Rachael to make up her own mind in this, as any concerned parent would. However, my faith was sorely torn in this situation, and it was difficult for me. When you left, Dilana, I considered that was an end to the matter. I was wrong." The sister shook her head. "So very wrong. The child pined for you, and we could do nothing but watch her deterioration. Even when you came back and tried to make amends for your absence, she was very upset. She cared for you as she had no other. Now, of course, it is clear why, but then I thought you and she were only friends, good friends."

"I told you I loved her," Rachael said.

Di took Rachael's hand and squeezed it gently. "We were—no still are—only friends, Sister. The depth of our friendship however, goes much deeper. Neither Rachael nor I would ever want to inflict any undue hurt on you, the orphanage, nor all the other nuns who help run the school."

Sister Angela turned and stared at them both. Facial tics indicated she was conflicted. Di wondered, not for the first time, what went through a nun's head when confronted with something that went against their ordered lives and religious beliefs. She had a feeling that she would know soon enough.

"Thank you for the consideration."

"I wanted your blessing, Sister. You are the most important person in my life, barring Dilana. I want you to approve and wish us well. I know it won't be easy, but if we know that we have the support of the ones who love us the most, we have a fighting chance."

Rachael's brilliant gaze implored her surrogate mother. Di observed the sudden relaxed stance from the two women and heaved a sigh of relief. She knew that she wouldn't have resisted the begging that oozed from Rachael.

"My child, in my heart you have always had my blessing. How can I deny the depth of affection you have shown? Now, you are willing to sacrifice what you love and have known the most, for her. However…"

A break through. "However?" Di asked quickly, not wanting to sound pushy, but any break in the deadlock was worth exploring. They might yet find their middle ground.

"The bishop will not approve. If he finds out that I have known all along and did nothing to try and convince you that it is wrong…well, let's just say my time here would be ended."

"Does the bishop have to know?" Di asked.

"If Rachael leaves here, he will be interested in her whereabouts and her well-being. When he finds out that she's moved in with you, I don't know what he might do."

"What he might do? How can he do anything? Rachael is free to choose her own life. Right?"

"Yes, Sister, Bishop Clarence can't do anything to me except…" Rachael gasped.

Staring into space for a few precious seconds, Di wondered if she would ever get used to people who never finished a sentence properly, especially an important one. "Except?"

"He will probably take steps to remove me from the school and my contact with the nuns—my family." Sister Angela shook her head.

"Can he do that?" Di looked from Sister Angela to Rachael.

Sister Angela nodded. "Yes, he can. Now, anyway, since we don't have a mother superior. Otherwise, he wouldn't have the need to see the structure of our everyday personnel or have a hand in running the school."

"I see. Are they going to appoint another one?"

Di saw Rachael give a nod at the Sister.

"He still wants me to take over."

Di felt a goofy grin settle on her face when she heard this. *Wow what a middle ground.* "There's an answer to both your prayers then, Sister. You take over as Mother Superior and Rachael doesn't have to be ostracized from her position or the church." The simplicity of the situation glared out at them and Di hoped they both would see it.

"Dilana, Sister doesn't want to be Mother Superior. I can't expect her to do something she doesn't want because of my selfish needs."

"Why? What is so odious about the job, Sister?" The reason astounded Di. She always thought moving up the ladder was a goal, even for nuns.

"Not so much odious, rather more meetings with the bishop. I have been considering the situation carefully for some time. Perhaps, if you will leave me, I'll reflect on it some more with my family here and give my final answer to the bishop?"

"Sure. I need to go back to the city for a couple of days. Maybe when I get back we can talk again." Di smiled at Sister Angela, who nodded before turning back to her contemplation of the garden area outside her window.

"The family does include Rachael, right?"

"I'm sorry, it is the nuns only."

"Do we have to worry?" Di sucked in a deep breath before the nun answered.

"If this is true love, does it matter?"

Di smiled. "It does not. This is true love, for sure."

Rachael grinned at her, and Sister Angela gave them a wink.

166

Chapter Thirteen

Di stood outside the new mother superior's office, and her heart swelled at what this could mean—no, must mean—to her relationship with Rachael. She had been away a week, and when Rachael called last night to say Sister Angela was now the mother superior, nothing SG could do would have stopped Di from making the journey home at once. She needed to talk to the nun. Rachael knew she was due home, and they had planned a private dinner at her house in the evening. She didn't want to go behind Racheal's back, but this conversation she needed to have alone with Sister Angela. Rachael was working anyway, and Di would be there when the school day was over and surprise Rachael.

A nun appeared out of nowhere. Di was sure she recalled her from the first time she'd ventured into the hallowed area of the nunnery, way back when. The nun gave Di a smile before indicating that she enter the door marked *Mother Superior*.

Di smiled and nodded then gave a tentative knock on the larger-than-life wooden door before opening it. She poked her head around the door and saw brown, intent eyes capture hers. "Is it safe to come inside, now that you are the head honcho and all?"

There was a soft chuckle. Di stepped inside, about to close the door, only to have a tall nun she was sure she had seen before enter behind her.

"Ah, Sister Faith. Have you ever been introduced to Ms. Sterling?"

Di watched the nun shuffle before bending her head to hide what she was sure were the nun's cheeks staining red.

"Of course, you wouldn't. How silly of me. Please, Dilana, let me introduce, Sister Faith. She's a devoted fan of your work, especially the latest. Isn't that right, Sister?"

Di turned to the obviously embarrassed nun who kept her head down but mumbled, "I enjoy your storytelling."

"Thank you. Now that I know I have a true fan here, perhaps you'd do me the honor of reading my next book when it goes through the final edits. I would like to know what you think."

"I…well, of course."

Di smiled and gave the nun her full attention. "Thank you. It means a lot to me."

The nun giggled then sheepishly looked at the mother superior.

"Give us fifteen minutes, and then remind me of my appointment with the bank. Thank you, Sister."

The nun nodded, and with a shy smile toward Di, she left the room.

"Thank you."

Di turned to the mother superior, lifted her hand, and smiled. "It's my pleasure. The more critics I have before publication, the better. Besides that, congratulations on your new position."

"Thank you. I've had the post all of two days, and I confess, it is quite intimidating."

Di frowned. "Didn't you do the vast majority of the work anyway, before you took the job?"

The nun shrugged and grinned, pointing to the seat opposite her at the desk. "Ah, but then I wasn't totally responsible. Now I am, and that makes a huge difference."

Di took the seat and nodded.

"To business, how can I help you, Dilana?"

Di chuckled. "Do I need to actually spell it out?"

The nun shook her head and returned the grin. "No, Rachael has been very vocal on the both of your behalves since I returned."

"I'm sorry. I know you must have a multitude of other, more important, problems to solve. Shall we table this for a better time?" Di knew that pressuring others didn't work.

The nun gazed at her intently. "My dear, there is nothing more important to me than Rachael and her happiness. Though, please do not express this outside our conversation. Regardless of what people think, nuns do have feelings, and family is paramount."

"I don't know what to say. You humble me."

"Good. Life, I've found over the years, is understanding the points of view of others and moving forward. I believe you have shown that, Dilana, and with that in mind…"

Di wanted to do the whole theatrical arms akimbo and raised eyebrows—you-left-me-in-limbo kind of look. Instead, she waited with what she hoped was a relaxed expression. There was silence for a while. "In mind?" Di desperately asked.

"Why, I approve of course."

Di ran around the desk and hugged the older woman close. "Thank you, thank you, thank you."

Di was pushed gently away. "My daughter loves you, and I believe you love her too. God moves in mysterious ways, I find. The one thing we all should strive for in life is loving our fellow man…or woman, and in my capacity as God's voice, I find to desecrate love is unacceptable."

"I totally understand why Rachael loves you as much as she does. Does this mean we can share a life together?" Di kind of knew the answer but was amazed at the response.

"I have one prerequisite."

"Okay, name it." Di held her breath, as she waited for the answer.

Mother Superior placed the tips of her fingers together and gave a somber expression.

Darn, what the hell is it? Di chewed down on her bottom lip.

"Would you consider marrying my daughter before you live together? I know it might not be to your—"

Di threw her arms around the nun and kissed her cheek. "Absolutely. My God, you didn't even need to go through the angst of asking."

"When do you think we can make the arrangements?

Di stroked her chin. *This is going to be hard.* Rachael thought that once Di came back from her city trip it would be moving in time. *Damn, how can I do this and not hurt her?* "Rachael thinks that we will live together basically when I get back. I guess I could delay my arrival, but that would mean another lie."

"No more lies between the two of you. If it will help, there is a teaching conference Rachael has been begging to attend. Funding has always been difficult, but I think I can divert funds for this cause. At the end of the day, it will benefit all parties. If she has changed her mind because of her new circumstances...then perhaps you can cajole her. Will that give us time to make the necessary arrangements?"

Di grinned. Sister Angela deserved to be Mother Superior. She was devious in a nice way to reach her goals. "Great idea. When is the conference and for how long?"

The nun laughed. "Starts the day after tomorrow. Rachael would need to travel tomorrow afternoon, and it's in, of all places, Alaska. The conference lasts four days."

"Alaska? Wow she'll be rubbing noses with Eskimos. Hmm, this will mean more time apart." Di twisted her lips. "We never seem to catch a break when it comes to being together."

"My dear, a little abstinence never hurt anyone."

Di rolled her eyes, "Yeah abstinence, I know all about that. I think in another life I was a nun."

They both laughed.

"If all goes according to plan, then we have a six-day window," Di said. "Is it doable?"

The nun laughed loudly. "With Mrs. D, you, and I, plus the hand of God at our side, it will be a piece of cake."

"SG will want to be involved. She adores Rachael." At the nun's raised eyebrows, Di clarified. "In a benign way, she is besotted with her new husband and wants everyone to be as happy as she is." Di gazed intently at Sister Angela, who might have a new title, but that hadn't clicked in yet. "Thank you, for everything."

"Welcome to the family, Dilana."

171

†

"It's got to be pink because nothing else is."

"Not happening, SG. A pink wedding cake doesn't compute. Why does it have to have any kind of pink anyway? I always thought anything to do with a wedding had to be white?" Di threw up her hands and walked a few steps to stand at the balustrade of the balcony looking down to the deserted beach. No Rachael. *I miss you so much, my love. I hope you are having a better time than I am.*

"I'm sure we can put some pink icing wording on the white-iced cake. Maybe the names. Would that work?"

Di turned to her partners in crime, or, perhaps in collusion. *God help me, I hope Rachael says yes.* "Excellent idea, Mrs. D. Where would we be without you to sort us out?" Di flicked a glance at Mother Superior who gave her a wink. "All of us, right?" Her eyes traversed the room.

Mother Superior rose out of her chair and nodded. "Perfect sense to me. As this is the last item on the agenda, do you mind if I excuse myself? I have a report to prepare for the bishop, and he intends to visit on Friday."

"Friday, is there a problem?" Di pierced Mother Superior with her eyes. A gentle hand settled on her arm, and she looked into an equally warm gaze.

"No, as it turns out, it's the yearly visit. With everything that has gone on in the last six months, I'd quite forgotten. The bishop would like to meet you personally, Di, if you are free—"

"Sorry, Sister…Mother. I'm afraid Di has promised me one last interview opportunity before she becomes a recluse from the public eye. She will be whisked away tomorrow afternoon and won't be back until late afternoon Friday."

Di frowned and remained silent.

"Ah well, another time perhaps. Now, I must go."

"Me too. My Bob will want his dinner on time as always. I'll take care of all the catering details and the town's people you want invited. Want me to drop you home, Mother?"

Di watched in fascination that four women so different in personality and lifestyles could, in such a short space of time, arrange what she knew would be a wonderful event. Now, all that was left was for the main participant in the affair to say one word and make it all happen. *Will she?*

✝

Mother Superior took in every inch of Rachael's appearance. She looked beautiful; from the glossy, chestnut hair held in a cream braid to the simple, yet stunning, line of the off-white dress. Her shoes matched perfectly with the outfit she wore.

"I still don't know where she's taking me, exactly, except she said I had to dress up and that we would meet at the beach house and go from there."

Rachael was staring at herself in the long mirror, at the clothes specially sent from a store in the city. By the price tags, she would have had to save for ten years to buy them herself. Dilana had insisted that this was important, and only the best was good enough for her girl.

"Perhaps, it's something to do with her book. You know she's due to pick up a literary award. Maybe it's that?" Mother Superior said.

"Hmmm. I don't think so. That's next month in New York, or so SG said at her last visit."

"Well, you will know soon enough. Now, come along, Rachael. I promised to drive you there and not to be late. She said noon and noon it will be."

Ten minutes later, she was being waved off by the two oldest nuns who had tears in their eyes as she climbed aboard the vehicle. Anyone would think she wasn't coming back.

As they drove up the small circular drive to the house, Rachael gasped at the bunting that adorned every available space. *What is going on?*

"Sister, is it someone's birthday and I've forgotten? Oh no, not Dilana's. It can't be, can it?" Her wits scattered, as she tried to recall the writer's birthday. She had said it was March. Rachael was certain of it.

The nun didn't respond and braked slowly, bringing the car to a stop. Sister Angela got out of the car quickly.

Rachael looked out the car window. Dilana, resplendent in a sky-blue, silk tuxedo, her short, blonde hair in a becoming style that not only complimented her face but the outfit too, was coming toward the car.

Unable to take her eyes off her, Rachael could only stare at the woman she loved totally. She watched, as Sister Angela spoke with Dilana and then headed off toward the house. Dilana walked to the car and opened the front passenger door, smiling nervously.

"Dilana?" Rachael whispered, wondering why the butterflies were mounting an attack in her stomach. She leered shamelessly at the writer.

Holding out her hand, Di gently helped her out of the car.

"Dilana?"

"You look beautiful, and you smell wonderful."

Glancing down at her clothes, Rachael had to admit she washed up good. "Thank you, and you look magnificent. Have I missed something important?"

"I'm glad you approve, Rachael, and no you haven't. I have something to ask you."

"Yes?"

"Will you be my life partner, and live with me here in the beach house?"

"Life partner? Is that similar to a proposal?" Her heart stuck in her mouth. She knew that was a ridiculous question. *Of course it is a proposal. How dumb can I be?*

"Yes, it is. Sorry." Dilana knelt in front of her and grinned. "Marry me?" Heaven came to both women, as Rachael gave her a stunning smile and reached down to tip Dilana's head and place small kisses all over her face. "YES, YES, YES." she shouted

Di swept her up in her arms, and they traded kiss for kiss for a few minutes, before Di placed Rachael gently back on the ground.

"In that case, if you would be so good as to step this way." Di led Rachael gently toward the side of the house and through the gate. Loud applause greeted them from the private beach made into an open-air sitting area with a small archway full to the brim with people from the town. SG and her husband were in the front row of the seating, Mother Superior sat next to them.

"I can't believe you arranged this without me knowing." Rachael gasped and felt herself shaking with nerves, as they proceeded toward the arch.

"It wasn't easy, but we have some very special friends."

Alan Forrester, a city vicar and friend of SG's, who had no problem with any repercussions from the church, carried out the ceremony with a sparkle in his eyes and a gentle smile constantly plastered over his lips.

When Alan asked Rachael, if she took this woman to be her lawfully wedded wife, she shyly gazed up at Dilana and saw a nervous smile. She returned one of her own.

"I do." That nervous smile disappeared like magic, and Di was asked the same.

"I do."

"I now pronounce you married. You may kiss the bride…brides." Alan winked, as Rachael was swept up in Dilana's arms and kissed thoroughly.

As the day ended, they were finally alone in the house, covered in confetti and so happy with how everything went. Rachael was sure they had permanent grins etched on their faces.

"I love you, Dilana, but you didn't need to do this."

"Oh, I did, darling, because I want you now and for always. The commitment was important to you, and I couldn't think of anything more committed than being married and proclaiming my love and future to you with all our friends there to support us. Well, almost all of our friends. I thought maybe we could have a special BBQ for some of the nuns unable to attend, and the kids of course, in a couple of weeks."

A tear splashed down Rachael's cheek, as she realized that life couldn't get any more wonderful. Or could it? She saw the passion flaring in the grey eyes of her soon-to-be lover.

"I will never forget today, Dilana, you have made me so happy."

Crushing Rachael close, Di sucked in a breath then said. "I don't know how I got so lucky to have you in my life, but by God, I'm going to make sure that I never stuff it up. You are my miracle, and I want to spend the rest of my life loving you if you will let me."

"Hmm sounds like a plan, as long as I can do the same."

"Absolutely, my love."

The passion that had been smoldering ignited into a giant flame that consumed them both.

Di drew away, "Let's go to bed."

†

Di sucked in a breath as she slipped under the sheets and felt Rachael's naked body next to hers. Never in her life had she been so turned on. She slipped her arm around Rachael's slender waist and snuggled close. "Is this okay?" she asked.

"Oh, it is more than okay. You are all I've ever wanted." She closed her eyes. "I have no experience, so you will have to teach me."

Di smiled. "With pleasure." She leaned in and kissed Rachael, her tongue asking for a deeper kiss, and Rachael parted her lips.

They both sighed.

Di broke away and gently caressed her lover's body. "You take my breath away," she said before kissing down the length of Rachael's body.

"Please, Dilana, I need more."

Di looked up and grinned before taking a taut nipple into her mouth.

Rachael's hand immediately went to Di's head and held her in place. She moaned deeply. "I had no idea," she whispered.

Lips, tongue, and fingers roamed over her body caressing her everywhere except the one place where Di knew she desperately needed touching.

"Please," Rachael begged again, "make me yours."

"Gladly. I love you so much."

"I love you too." Rachael pulled Dilana close. "I've dreamed of you all my life. I knew it was you from the moment you stood next to me on the beach."

With tenderness, Di explored every inch of Rachael's body with her fingers and lips. When her touch elicited moans from her soon-to-be lover, Di felt a joy that she'd never known. She wasn't having sex. For the first time in her life, she was making love. Never before did she care about another's satisfaction, her own had been the only one that mattered.

Until now.

With tenderness, she caressed Rachael's velvety wetness, being careful not to push too hard. It was Rachael's first time, and the last thing she wanted was to hurt her. She slid her finger in gently, only to be surprised when muscles squeezed hard and began gently drawing her in deeper. Her thumb automatically began rubbing the engorged clitoris, and Rachael's hips began rocking while she moaned in what sounded like pleasure.

Di gasped when Rachael's finger slid inside her, mimicking her movements. Soon, they were as one moving together. Di was amazed when they screamed out their orgasm at the same moment. There were a few moments of sheer wonder at the emotion of the moment.

Wrapped in Rachael's arms and deliriously happy, Di sighed. "I love you Rachael, my beautiful bride. Never in my life has anyone ever elicited the feelings you do inside me."

Rachael raised on one elbow and looked at her with a raised eyebrow. "I know I'm not the first woman you've been with. I bet you've lost count on how many."

Di closed her eyes. It was a valid question, but one she didn't want to taint this moment. When would it ever be the right time? She snuggled closer to Rachael's breast, kissing the milky white flesh, and heard the throaty indrawn breath. "You are right, I can't even begin to come to a number, but know this, Rachael, I've never made love to any of them. They were just bodies to give me satisfaction. You are the only one I've ever loved or cared about."

"Really?" Rachael's voice was full of wonderment.

"Yes. I love you so much, I think my heart will burst, it is so full." She nuzzled further into the delectable breast close to her lips. "Just when I think I can't love you more, you look at me and smile, and I am overcome with even more love."

Rachael smiled and kissed her shoulder. "I love you too." She ran a finger between Di's breasts down to her navel. "Can we do it again?"

Di leaned in and kissed Rachael's lips. "For the rest of our lives. My daughter of Poseidon, my wife."

Chapter Fourteen

"It's a wonderful sight isn't it, Mother?" SG asked.

Sister Angela nodded. "Yes, it is, my child. Yes, it is."

They both watched the youngsters running about on the beach laughing and playing as many games as they could. There was also the usual contingent of locals helping to provide the BBQ feast that had become a tradition for the last Saturday of every month. Surprisingly enough, more people were joining in and bringing their own kids along to a very community-spirited event these days.

SG spotted Di alone at the edge of the beach. Gentle waves were lapping her feet, as she stood there gazing at the horizon. SG had learned of this ritual of Di's, having spent the last few days discussing the new book project and a new contract. She excused herself and headed toward her friend.

"Penny for them?"

Spinning around with a faraway expression on her face, Di looked at her with a faint smile. "Oh, I think they are worth more than that, SG. They are memories. Very precious memories."

"Care to share any?" She suspected she knew exactly that those memories were of a certain woman who was mute when the memories were being created.

"No. Do I ask you about your memories?"

"Nope, however you can if you like. We could always call this evening a slumber party and share our girly secrets. What do you say?" SG laughed at the surprise on Di's face. She was so gullible.

"Don't be silly, SG." Di looked toward the boisterous children on the beachfront beside her villa.

"I wonder if, when they grow up, they'll venture out again to the sea." SG softly said. Her eyes followed Di's to Sam and Sadie. They had nearly drowned on their foolish adventure, six months earlier. Now, they were running about without a care in the world. Fortunately, kids had resilient characteristics that prevented them from dealing with what might have been. Had Di and Rachael not been around to save their lives, things would have turned out very differently. "Well, if they don't go in the actual sea, I know, for certain, they will end up challenging the sea of life. They are full of questions wanting answers. I wonder how the orphanage copes with them sometimes."

"They have wonderful, caring people who love them as their own. That makes quite a difference." SG linked her arm with her friend's, as she too stared out toward the horizon. It was a calm ocean scene, showing none of its ability to quickly change its mind like a jealous lover. "Why do you look out there? It never changes anything."

"Fate, SG, fate. It has brought me great joy and sorrow, and I wonder at the unpredictability of it all. I guess, at the end of the day, nature is telling us never to forget that life can be unpredictable and that you must take your chances when you have the opportunity. Never regret anything, because you can't go back and change it."

SG squeezed Di's arm. As shown in her recent works, she was becoming quite the mature author. Even her recent children's book held a message in a very subtle way.

"Darryl has a month off in October, and we were going to take a trip to the Far East. Want to come along?"

"You're going?"

"Yeah, why not?" SG grinned at the astonished look on her friend's face. SG knew why Di was asking the question but was waiting to see what she said.

"Well I thought maybe—that is, you know?"

SG smiled at her friend and winked. "I do, but the last time I checked, being six months pregnant isn't a valid reason for not traveling."

"Will they allow you to fly? I know I wouldn't. What does Darryl say?"

"Oh, Ms. Worry Wart, the doc says I'm healthy, and Darryl has a doctor's name ready and able at each destination. All I can say is, I'm glad I'm not married to you."

Di shook her head. "No chance of that." She smirked.

"Come on, let's join the others. Otherwise, we will be called antisocial."

"Yeah, let's."

†

Di smiled at her reflection in the mirror. Having showered and changed, she felt relaxed. The day had gone well. It was late in the year for BBQs, but no one seemed to want to stop the events. They had all agreed that they would continue until the weather changed dramatically.

As she pondered that thought, she recalled SG's invitation to join her and Darryl on their trip to the Far East. An area of the globe she hadn't traveled was tempting but—

Hands placed around her waist stopped her train of thought, as she was engaged in rather more pleasurable activities. Kisses rained down her neck, and a voice she would never get tired of hearing whispered, "I love you."

"I love you too. Want to know how much?"

That giggle always sent the blood running through her veins notching up a degree or two. She grinned and turned in the hold, reversing the role, and held the woman who had sneaked in from her shower. Di dipped her head to kiss the lips that now could speak.

"I know, you show me constantly." Rachael huskily replied.

"Ah, I think you deserve more." Di captured the luscious lips once more. Life couldn't get better in her view. She had a woman at her side that she loved to distraction and who miraculously loved her with the same depth. They had a wonderful life here on the beach, and her work was acclaimed and in demand, providing an income that allowed them to indulge their other passion. The orphanage.

As she stared down into the azure eyes, she was reminded of how close it had been that day, six months ago, when things might have been so different.

†

"No," Dilana shouted in a strangled way, as she heard Sam reminding Rachael about Ben. Whoever the hell Ben was, she was sure it wasn't another child.

183

"I can save Ben, Dilana. Trust me." Rachael hoarsely said, as she turned in the direction of the small object bobbing out of reach.

"Don't. Please, don't. You are too tired. What would I do without you?"

Rachael looked at the object and turned back toward the shore, allowing the wave to take Ben and push her closer to shore.

Minutes later, they were on the beach. Mrs. D fussed over Sam, as Dilana left him in her charge to help Rachael out of the water. Emotions ran high, as she hugged the woman close and whispered in her saltwater soaked hair. "I would be beyond help if anything had happened to you, Rachael. God knows, I love you."

Rachael gave a tired smile, her eyes sparkled, and she moved closer to Dilana.

"I love you too, Dilana. Do you think we can start again?" Her voice rasped, and she relaxed like a rag doll into Di's arms.

"Oh, yes, my love. Try and stop me. Can I ask one more thing?"

"Sure," Rachael's voice sounded hoarse.

"Who is Ben that you would put yourself in more danger?"

Rachael sighed and gave a tight smile. "Ben was the only possession that Sam had from his birth mother. A rather raggedly looking bear, but for Sam, a reminder that he was once part of a family. I understood his need to save the object."

Di sucked in a deep breath. "He will always be part of a family, Rachael...ours. We can replace the bear but not you, and that might have been the sacrifice."

"I know. I'm sorry."

"Never be sorry, my love, for caring. Let's go home."

As they gathered up the children, Di bent down to pick up Rachael's discarded clothes and the note that lay there in the sand. Rachael watched her.

"Dilana."

"Yeah?"

"The note you have in your hand, will you throw it in the sea?"

Puzzled but too tired to argue, she did exactly that. They both watched it bounce around until it was swallowed by a large wave, its contents never to be seen again.

"Come on, let's go home." Di lead Rachael by the arm toward the beach house.

"Yes, home sounds perfect with you."

†

Di smiled and stroked Rachael's hair. "SG asked if we wanted to go traveling the Far East with her and Darryl in the autumn. What do you think?"

"The Far East? Wow, I've never been out of the States. It would be wonderful. Oh—what about my work at the school?"

Di decided there and then that they would go. She had been debating the issue herself. She wasn't that keen on going out of the country ever again after cruising the Mediterranean with Celina. "We can arrange a replacement. It's time the school had another teacher, and we did talk about this when we got married."

"We did, didn't we? With everything that's gone on these past few months, I guess it slipped our minds. Shall we arrange to talk with Sister Angela about it?"

Di chuckled, as she hugged Rachael to her chest "You'll never get used to calling her Mother Superior, will you?"

"Oh no. I did it again, didn't I? I guess she will always be Sister Angela to me. I think she did the right thing in taking the post though. Heck, she's quite celebrated at the bishop's dinner when she goes to the city once a month."

"Why?" Di frowned. This was something new. She'd never heard about it before.

"Because of you."

"Me?"

"Yep, the bishop was asking her, only last month, if there was a chance that she might bring you along with her. They are all dying to meet you." Rachael chuckled.

"Don't be silly. I'm not a suitable guest for a bishop's monthly dinner party. Whatever would they make of a dyke like me?" Di self-consciously shrugged off the possibility.

"Why, Di, I do believe that you are embarrassed." Rachael trailed a finger down Di's burnt cheekbones.

Capturing the errant finger, she kissed the digit gently and pulled Rachael as close as she possibly could. "I don't get embarrassed. I leave that to others."

"Really? Well then I'll tell Sis—Mother Superior that you will gladly attend."

Di shook her head at the teasing she was being subjected to. "Yeah. If I go, so do you."

"I'm not going. They don't want me around."

"They might not. However, I do. Anywhere I go, you do too. Simple really, and anyway, they get a bargain, two for the price of one."

A silence stretched out for a couple of minutes. "You know we can't go together." The softly spoken words reminded Di of the pact they had made with Sister Angela.

"Yeah, I remember. Maybe, I should go with Mother Superior to enlighten Bishop Clarence. Who knows, he might come around." Laughing, she saw the twinkle in her lover's eyes.

"I love you, Dilana, so very much. I'm glad that it worked out for us." A faraway look settled on Rachael's face.

"Want to tell me what made you suddenly so pensive?" Di gently tilted Rachael's head so she could plant a soft kiss at the corner of her mouth.

"I was wondering what our life would be like if we had to go it alone without everyone who's been so supportive?"

Di didn't answer immediately. She sucked in a deep breath and smiled as she hugged the woman she loved closer. The hug was as close as she could get without preventing her from breathing. "Sometimes, Rachael, it's best not to dwell on what might have been and just thank our lucky stars that all the good things we are experiencing last a lifetime."

Looking up she saw the love that brimmed from those often-serious, grey orbs. Yes, Dilana was right; why worry about something that never was and now never would be? She indeed had been blessed in many ways and none more so than Dilana's surprise the weekend after Sister Angela became Mother Superior. Their secret wedding, except it wasn't secret to anyone but her. There had been a moment of confusion, and perhaps anger, that one of the most important days of her life had been arranged without her knowledge. It was a fleeting moment though, as she saw the joy on Dilana's face when she entered the private beach and there was a round of applause from the guests. The day had been perfect in every way, a day she would never forget for all the right reasons.

"I think you are right and I'd rather dwell on pleasanter thoughts."

"Would you know how I could make that happen?" Di wriggled her eyebrows in an exaggerated fashion and Rachael giggled.

Tender arms held her close and she reveled in how it was to be loved like this. She had found someone special enough to look beyond her faults and see into her heart, and for this woman, it was solid gold love. "How about I tell SG that we will travel with them? We can always give them the slip from time to time."

"Oh, Dilana, that sounds as if we don't want to spend time with them." Laughing softly, she said, "It is a rather wonderful idea."

"Yeah well, I don't. Not all the time. It can be our honeymoon. We never did get away, did we?"

"No, we didn't, and I think that's a wonderful idea. Let's go for a walk on the beach before bed. We can tell SG in the morning."

"Marvelous idea, darling." They released each other but walked as close as possible out of the house, eventually entwining arms, as they walked along the moonlit beach. A while later, they ended up at the one spot they could both find if they were blind.

"I will never forget the first time I saw you standing here." Di breathed into Rachael's hair, drinking in the woman's perfume and the sea air.

"I'll never forget the first time I saw you too."

"Really, care to share?"

Rachael laughed and snuggled into the arms that held her tightly. "You told me that I was the small, silent type. When I looked at you, I think I fell in love in that single moment. You looked so cute and out of control."

"You remember the words I said to you that day?"

"Oh yeah. It was the best chat up line ever after you failed with 'beautiful day.'" Rachael giggled, as she saw the astonishment in her wife's eyes. "Let me see now, yeah. 'I guess you're the silent type, huh?'"

"I can't believe you remember the exact words. My God, darling, you are amazing." Di bent her head to snatch a kiss, which ended up as a longer exploration.

"Okay, I've told you mine, now it's your turn."

"Well—would you believe the first time I saw you convinced me that this was the place to be? You were the deciding factor in me taking this house when I saw you standing alone, watching the ocean. I figured you must be a part of nature, my love, or so I thought at the time. Still do sometimes when you go all quiet on me as you stare out to sea. It's about the only time you leave me, and I miss you, but I also know you will be back."

Rachael felt the arms around her pull her close to prevent her leaving physically. They'd discussed that aspect of her mental state. She might have recaptured her voice, but the sea had cruelly taken her parents. The memories and heartache remained. A very tender moment on the day of their wedding created a different sort of memory…

†

"Rachael, there's one more thing I'd like to do, if it's okay with you?" Di whispered.

"Anything for you, Dilana, you know that." Rachael, smiling in joy, felt this had been one wonderful day and it kept getting better.

Di picked up the large spray of flowers that had been presented to Rachael as they stood under the arch with the vicar. Di had managed to stop Rachael from throwing it to some of the single people there, because she had what she hoped would be a fitting place for the spray.

Walking together, hand in hand, they approached the place where they had met for the first time.

"I'd like us to throw the spray into the sea, in memory of your parents. I hope that if they are looking over us, they will approve of what we pledged today." Di was tentative, she knew how much Rachael still mourned her parents' passing and always probably would have that small niggling doubt that she could have done more to help them.

There was no sound for a few moments, then Di heard a small sob and bent her head to look at the face of the woman she adored. Had it been a bad choice? Damn, what a way to end a beautiful day, was she so dense that—?

"I think it's a beautiful idea, Dilana, thank you."

Holding out her hand for the spray, Rachael quietly spoke a few words and tossed it into the ocean.

"They know I love you, Dilana, and you love me. How can they not be happy for us?" Smiling through her emotional tears, Rachael pulled down Di's head and passion quickly overcame every other thought.

†

"I'll always come back to you, Dilana. You are my life, now and always."

Dilana sighed happily. How her life had changed in two short years. She knew that, someplace, her dad was watching with her mom, and they would approve of how her life had turned around. She certainly did.

"I know you will come back, love. Even in silence, I feel your love for me, and I know it always will be. You are my special daughter of Poseidon."

Laughing at the thought, they walked back toward the house and the rest of their lives. "Did you really get the idea of your book *In Search of Poseidon's Daughter* from me?"

"Who else, my love?"

As the sea gently lapped the shore, two very happy women turned their backs for the evening, but they would be back. They always came back. Poseidon never turned his back on his daughter, now he'd gained another, and there was always room for one more child of the sea.

About the Author

JM Dragon

JM Dragon is a New Zealand citizen, living in the beautiful Canterbury countryside. She loves to garden, travel, write, take care of her animals and family, and pursue her business interests—Affinity eBook Press and a Canterbury manufacturing company.

She is a keen reader of sci-fi, crime/mystery, classics, and romance, which help to feed her imagination for her own stories.

Currently published by Affinity eBook Press NZ LTD, her books include *The Promise, Do Dreams Come True, Fix-it Girl, In Name Only, The Destiny Series, Circus,* and 2015 GCLS winner *The One.*

You can contact JM by:
email: jm1dragon@yahoo.com
or
Facebook: http://www.facebook.com/julie.dragon.

Other Books from Affinity eBook Press

Pausing by Renee MacKenzie

Jordy Chapman is the Emergency Service Coordinator at Cypress Haven mental health facility in Naples, FL. Keira Yeager's family owns an upscale furniture store in Naples and orchestrates a generous donation of furniture to Cypress Haven. When the two meet, they hit it off immediately. Will a Yeager family's anguish and misunderstanding threaten their new relationship?

The Termination by Annette Mori

Codee is having a bad day and it's only going to get worse. Sawyer, a compassionate young woman, is resigned to her fate. After slipping on ice, Codee wonders if she is hallucinating and fallen into an Alice type rabbit hole. The only thing she knows is that she needs to save Sawyer. Enjoy this satirical romance, with all of its twists and turns, that just might make you go hmm...

Next Time by Erin O'Reilly
What if you had the chance to make history stop repeating itself? Would you sacrifice today for a chance at a better tomorrow. There is a moment in everyone's life that defines their future. For Jac and Carol, that time is now. Jump ahead twenty-five years and meet Carol's granddaughter Livvy. She is ready for a challenge and is fleeing the nest and getting on with her life. Read this wonderful love story that spans several lifetimes.

Open Your Heart, a Sensual Collection by Ali Spooner
Excite your senses, rejuvenate your memories, and best of all, flirt with the edge of eroticism. Allow us to help you relive that first kiss, flirting with young love, your dream come true, surprise encounters, and your wildest desires... Enjoy these stories of love, sweet seduction, and steamy encounters. Open Your Heart...a sensual collection.

Secret of Stone Creek by Natalie London
Jennifer Cameron arrives in Stone Creek, Wisconsin to sell her grandparents' large Victorian home. While there, she is intrigued by a twenty-four-year-old never-solved murder. Her attraction to the lovely and mysterious librarian, Diana, vies for her attention. Follow this suspenseful whodunit to its conclusion.

The Promise by JM Dragon
An accidental meeting with Melissa Grant leads to an unexpected offer for Kris Lake—refurbishing a beach cottage with the help of Melissa's granddaughter, Claire. Do outer imperfections prevent them from reaching the beauty

that lives inside and the chance of a happy new life? Find out in this lovely romance that will fill you with heartwarming sensations throughout the story.

Christmas at Winterbourne by Jen Silver
The Christmas festivities for the guests booked into Winterbourne House have all the goings-on of a traditional holiday. The only difference is that this guesthouse is run by lesbians, for lesbians. Join the guests and staff at Winterbourne for a Christmas you'll not soon forget.

The Review by Annette Mori
Silver Lining, a successful lesbian romance writer, has the crazy idea to sponsor a contest where the first reader who posts a review wins a home-cooked meal with an offer to fly the winner to Washington State. Jasmine, the winner, has engaged in subtle flirtations with Silver. Bizarre messages from the unknown fan have Silver questioning the wisdom of a relationship with Jasmine.

South of Heaven by Ali Spooner
Kendra Drake has taken over as Captain of her father's shrimp boat. As a favor to her father, Kendra has agreed to give fellow shrimper, Lindsey Bowen, a chance to work on the boat but insists she must first prove herself to Kendra and her crew. Lindsey finds a way into Kendra's heart. Will it only last for the summer?

Catch to Release by Lacey Schmidt
On the verge of success, lesbian folk-rock star, Shay Greenaura, finds herself caught up in more than just her music. Threats have her manager hiring a security firm for protection. Addison Weller, a former Diplomatic Security

Services agent is called in to assess the threats against Shay. Their undeniable attraction, brewing silently between them, could prove to be a fatal distraction. Follow this fast-paced adventure to its surprising, romantic conclusion.

Ready for Love by Erin O'Reilly
Kylie Wilcox's life dramatically changed with the death of her husband. Dr. LJ Evans, a renowned archaeologist, needed and wanted nothing but her work for her happiness. Their worlds are about to collide and lives will be altered forever.

Neptune's Ring by Ali Spooner
In the sequel to *Venus Rising*, Nat and Liz, owners of Venus Rising, invite Levi and Vanessa to join them in a venture for a new club on another island. They find the perfect place in an unfinished resort, Neptune's Ring. While on the island, Levi is drawn into a mystery involving secret compartments and a murder. Join the characters in this page-turning adventure, filled with steamy romance, intrigue, and an unsolved murder.

The Ultimate Betrayal by Annette Mori
Lara is a successful, beautiful, charming, financier. She is also a total control freak, so whatever Lara wants, Lara makes sure she gets. Rachel is Lara's fun-loving, charming, irresistible wife. Sophia's surprise visit to see Lara sets in motion a number of life-changing events for them all. Hell has no fury as a woman scorned.

It's in Her Kiss by Various Affinity Authors
A collection of various holiday stories dedicated to anyone and everyone that reads it. Young, old, lesbian, gay, bisexual, and transgender. We are all the same inside and want the

same things outside...love, happiness, and that special someone to spend all of our holidays with.

Keeping Faith by TJ Vertigo
You loved them in the previous novels, Private Dancer, Reece's Faith, and Reece's Star, now join the antics of Reece, Faith, Cori, Vi, and even The Animal, one last time in *Keeping Faith*.

Bound by Ali Spooner
A rogue, master vampire threatens the existence of the New Orleans vampire clan. Lord Jordan enlists Devin Benoit, sister of the Baton Rouge Alpha, and her witch lover, Tia, to assist with cleansing the city from potential disaster.

The Circle Dance by Jen Silver
Jamie Steele has moved to another town, trying to forget the heartbreak of losing her lover of six years. Sasha Fairfield finds her thoughts taken up with her ex-lover and thinks she wants Jamie back. Follow this captivating romance, as love dances through the lives of these women, to its surprising conclusion.
hunt them. Immerse yourself in this fast-paced, romantic thriller by debut author Natalie London.

Take Me As I Am by JM Dragon & Erin O'Reilly
When Jo Lackerly and Thea Danvers meet, an unexpected friendship develops, proving a catalyst for both women to change their lives irrevocably. Follow them on a journey of discovery that will have your heart smiling, blood boiling, and senses entangled in a wonderful romance.

Print, E-Books, Free e-books

Visit our website for more publications available online.

www.affinityebooks.com

Published by Affinity E-Book Press NZ LTD
Canterbury, New Zealand

Registered Company 2517228